U.S.S.
MUDSKIPPER

U.S.S.
MUDSKIPPER

*The Submarine That
Wrecked a Train*

⚓ A NOVEL BY

William M. Hardy

DODD, MEAD & COMPANY
NEW YORK

Library of Congress Catalog Card Number: 67-12714

Printed in the United States of America
by Vail-Ballou Press, Inc., Binghamton, N. Y.

To Melissa and Peter

U.S.S.
MUDSKIPPER

Jonathan Tolliver, Commander of the U. S.S. Mudskipper stationed off the coast of Hokkaido near the end of World War II, cracks under the strain of his sixth mission and formulates an unheard of commando action for his bored and inactive crew - an attempt to destroy a Japanese freight train.

One

⚓

THE LOCOMOTIVE was a thing apart from its surroundings. Gleaming with paint and polish, fashioned out of steel and brass and pride, it awaited the guiding, dedicated touch of the man, Inouye—because the locomotive and Inouye were one, a fused entity of metal and flesh. They lived as one, and it was inevitable that they would one day die as one.

On the morning in June of 1945, in the gray sodden world which was the railway station of Nemuro, the locomotive was the only object possessed of any brightness or life. It had rained all through the night, and within a few hours it would undoubtedly rain again. The section of Nemuro in which the station was located typified the rest of that town—marked with narrow, muddy streets which were crowded with a people whose faces bore the stamp of a stolid recognition of defeat in a war with an enemy they neither knew nor understood. These people moved through the streets slowly, wearily, without purpose.

1

They talked very little and then in soft, dispirited voices. There was no laughter. Hanging over and all around the gray silent people and the gray unpainted buildings was the morning fog—shrouding the scene, enveloping the grayness within its own consummate gloom to work an elaborate tapestry of despair.

Except for one thing—except for the locomotive.

The locomotive was not new. It had been built in the late 1920s in the busy locomotive plants of Kobe on the main island of the Empire, Honshu. After many years of service on the Rokaido Main Line, running between Kobe and Tokyo, the locomotive had been sent to the northern island of Hokkaido for use on the newly constructed line connecting the little fishing port of Nemuro with the city of Kushiro which was the metropolis of eastern Hokkaido and the only port of any real consequence in the region. Now, due to the hardships imposed by the war, the tracks along that line were generally in a sorry state of repair. The countryside through which the line ran was, in its way, as depressing as Nemuro itself. The rolling stock pulled by the locomotive was ancient and dilapidated, but the locomotive—in a world characterized by leaden despair—remained a symbol of hope.

On this June morning the locomotive's train consisted of two wooden passenger cars and a dozen freight cars, also of wood. These freight cars had already been loaded with crates of fish and fish products—mostly sardine and salmon and tunny. Nemuro had little else to contribute to the Emperor and his shattered war machine. The workers who had loaded the freight cars were old men who now squatted on their aged haunches or stood near the train, awaiting one of the two events of their day which possessed any real significance for them—the departure of the train for Kushiro. The other event would be the train's return shortly before midnight. Then these same workers would unload the freight cars and reload them for the next day's run. And between the departure and the return of the train, their old men's lives stretched drearily and endlessly into an eternity of nothingness.

On this morning there were only a few passengers, most of them already aboard, sitting stiffly and silently on the wooden benches which extended the lengths of the cars. Their meager belongings were tied up in cloth bundles. Only one passenger still remained outside the train on the rotting planks of the station platform. His name was Kojima, a soldier whose home was in Nemuro and who had the great good fortune to have been assigned to ride as a guard on the train beteen Nemuro and Kushiro. It was a formality without any real significance, because on Inouye's train there could be no authority other than that of Inouye. However, it was a rule that there should be a military guard on every train which carried important cargo, and the food was important, so Kojima had been given the assignment. In reality, he rode the train just as any passenger would ride it. He had no contact with Inouye, who resented his presence, but he carried a gun with him, and, most important, he was able to visit for a few hours each morning with his family. With him on this morning stood his wife who held their infant son in her arms. Beside them was their daughter who was four. The family waited together silently, having no words to speak at this time of parting, but reluctant to relinquish the physical fact of being a family which was, for brief hours, together. Kojima stared impassively at the face of his wife from whose warm bed and arms he had separated himself half an hour earlier. There was much between him and this woman, but little of it ever found expression in words.

At precisely ten minutes before the hour of seven, a man emerged from the station building. He was small in stature, but there was about him an air of authority and assurance which made him appear larger than any of the men who watched him. Like the locomotive toward which he moved with a brisk, sure step, this man stood apart from his surroundings. He wore what looked to be a military uniform, although there was no insignia on either his neatly pressed blouse or his cap. In one hand he carried a pair of gloves and, in the other, a folded sheaf of papers.

The man was Inouye, and the locomotive was his locomotive. He was the engineer.

The old men watched him, their eyes lighting briefly. The soldier, Kojima, watched him. No one spoke to him, nor did he speak to any person. When he reached the locomotive he stopped for a moment and stood looking up at it. Then, slowly and with great care, he walked all around it, making his regular inspection. When he had found everything on the exterior of the locomotive to his satisfaction, he nodded his head in silent approval and drew on his gloves. Watching him, the old men repeated his confirmation of the locomotive's state of readiness, nodding their heads also. Inouye's putting on of his gloves was a ceremony, a fact of which he was fully aware. The ceremony completed, he pulled himself up into the locomotive's cab with a quick movement, paying no attention to the fireman, a bulky, grimy, discouraged-looking man named Tomiji who lurked near the firebox and leaned on his shovel. Tomiji already had a full head of steam up in the boiler. Inouye took this for granted. It would have been unthinkable for Tomiji not to have had steam up when the engineer arrived.

Inouye's watch, a fine one with a gold case, hung by a leather strap near the controls. The glance at that watch was pure ritual. He *knew* the time without having to check, and he *knew* his train would depart the Nemuro station on schedule. With Inouye's train there was no other authority to give the word for departure. When the time came, Inouye started his train. This was a simple fact, understood by all concerned.

On the platform, Kojima understood this and knew the time had come for him to board the train. He had already gone through the motions of checking the condition of the loaded freight cars. His wife understood also, and her hand touched the shoulder of their daughter. The little girl held out a parcel, wrapped in paper and tied with a string, to her father. In the parcel there was food for his journey, and he accepted it with a grave bow. It was a great and important gift.

Inside the cab of the locomotive, Inouye's gloved hands reached for and touched the gleaming handles of the controls. Slowly, with a kind of patient majesty, the wheels of the locomotive began to turn. Exhaust steam hissed from the cylinders as the connecting rods were thrust forward in eccentric paths by the movement of the pistons. With a series of laborious jerks, the ancient cars were urged into motion, and the day's run to Kushiro was under way—on schedule.

In the passenger cars, men and women sat stiffly, their masks of faces betraying neither interest nor emotion. Kojima sat with his back to the dirty window through which he might have watched his wife and children who still stood on the platform. He did not turn, keeping his eyes straight ahead. One hand held his automatic rifle. In his

5

lap, barely touched by the tips of the fingers of his other hand, was the parcel of food which his daughter had presented him.

In the locomotive's cab, Inouye watched impassively, almost disdainfully, as his train passed by the miserable wooden shacks on either side of the tracks. Then, suddenly, they were clear of the town in open country, and, as the squalor of Nemuro vanished behind him, Inouye opened the throttle to gain speed. For Inouye this was the point where his dream began to take form. The fog was lifting a bit, and this fact became a part of his dream— a symbol of the essence of his dream. He was able to forget the awful wretched squalor of Nemuro. He was able to forget the shabby, shameful cars which he pulled behind him. Inouye and his locomotive became free things— limitless in power, unhampered—a single, shining creature which was controlled by his will and the sure touch of his hand.

Then, as by a miracle, the coast was in sight. It was at this instant that Inouye realized the full impact of his dream—when the sea appeared. He was the master of a great ship, gleaming and proud and invincible. The sea was his proper home, he knew, and he leaned forward, his nostrils flaring as he strained to catch the first clean smell of the salt water. Then the train was moving along the coastline, and Inouye's face lighted with a smile of pure pleasure.

He saw the boy. The boy was not really a part of his dream, but he helped identify it, because the boy was always there—standing on the rock between the tracks and the sea as the train made its turn to follow the coast. And the boy always lifted one hand in salute. The salute seemed to say to Inouye, "I hereby admit you to your

6

dream." He was only a boy, small and poorly dressed—probably from a nearby farm. His pinched face appeared never to have known a smile, but he was, in his way, as faithful to Inouye's train as Inouye himself. Looking back, the engineer saw the tiny figure still standing, his hand still raised in that mute salute.

Then, down on the beach, Inouye saw a group of men straggling along, their heads down. His lips curled in contempt. He knew what those men were—a ragtail collection of farmers who had been formed into a home guard charged with patrolling the coast. They did not raise their eyes as his train passed them by. Their eyes, Inouye thought contemptuously, were turned forever downward toward the miserable dry land to which they were bound. One gloved hand reached for the control of the locomotive's whistle and pulled it—once, twice, three times—releasing the long, exultant scream of the whistle as Inouye's own cry of derision to the home guard—as his thanks to that small faithful boy—and as his personal salutation to the eternal sea for which he yearned.

And, as Inouye's train rattled along the Hokkaido coastline, black smoke belching from its stack, the cry of its whistle was noted by the small boy whose name was Takeo Nagumo. He lowered his hand but remained quite still and watched until the train was out of sight. The men in the home guard, led by an old man named Kurita, also heard the whistle, but they did not look up.

And all the while, the progress of Inouye's train was being watched by a man who could see the train and the smoke, but who could not hear the whistle.

Framed in the eye of the submarine's periscope, the train looked unreal—a toy train crawling past an artificial landscape. And, in a way, Commander Jonathan Tolliver saw it and thought of it as a toy. Tolliver stood hunched over the periscope in the conning tower of the U.S.S. *Mudskipper*, watching the progress of the train along the distant coastline with a fierce intensity which was typical of the man in times of stress. He had not spoken a word since he had taken over the periscope several minutes earlier, and when the *Mudskipper*'s Commanding Officer was silent, all hands in his immediate vicinity were likewise silent. As a result the conning tower had about it an air of solemnity which Wes Clayton found decidedly uncomfortable.

Clayton was the submarine's Executive Officer. It had been Clayton who had called Jonathan Tolliver to the conning tower to see the train, and he had done this without any idea of its being anything other than a curious diversion. Lieutenant Commander Wesley Clayton, a stocky, sandy-haired man—unimaginatively cheerful of disposition and highly efficient in the performance of routine tasks—considered the train something which might momentarily break the monotony of a patrol which had become deadly dull. Now, as he watched Tolliver's slender, wiry body bent over the periscope's eyepiece, Clayton was uneasily aware that his C.O. was really concentrating on that train. He could tell by the way Tolliver's hands gripped the training handles of the scope. They were remarkable hands—the hands of a surgeon, perhaps, strong and sure—and the knuckles showed white as they gripped the handles.

Hell, Wes Clayton thought, it's nothing but a Jap train. What's the old man got the wind up for?

But he did not consider questioning Tolliver. Jonathan Tolliver was a legend in his own time, and men who were legends were not to be questioned. Instead, Clayton simply watched his Commanding Officer, impressed as he always was by the electric quality of excitement the man was able to generate simply by his physical presence. In Clayton's basic and uncomplicated mind, Tolliver assumed godlike proportions, and the Executive Officer was given to studying Tolliver in the way men study their gods—seeing him in bold, simple, larger-than-life strokes—and accepting his actions regardless of an inability to comprehend them.

Tolliver spoke without removing his eye from the periscope. "Get Jake up here."

Clayton moved quickly to the intercom. "Mr. Stock to the conning tower!" He resented the order just as he resented the husky young officer who appeared on the ladder from below within seconds after he had been summoned. Lieutenant (jg) Jake Stock, the *Mudskipper's* Torpedo and Gunnery Officer possessed something Wes Clayton knew he would never have—the easy intimacy with Jonathan Tolliver which was born of five war patrols and the shared perils and triumphs of those patrols.

"Come here, Jake. I want you to see this." Tolliver straightened and moved aside as Stock, after a curious glance at Clayton, bent over the eyepiece of the periscope.

Alone in the submarine's regular complement of officers, Jake Stock was a mustang, a man who had come up through the enlisted ranks to receive a commission. Tolliver had put Stock in for that commission after their last patrol together—a patrol in which Stock had risked his life to clear a torpedo which had been stuck in its tube after failing to fire during an attack on a Japanese ship. Now he was Tolliver's man, and Wes Clayton knew it. So did every other officer on the submarine.

Stock straightened and glanced at Tolliver. The two men provided a marked contrast. Stock loomed huge and solid while Tolliver seemed fashioned like a fine rapier.

"How about that, Jake?"

Stock shrugged. "A train, Captain. It's not something you expect to see."

"No." Tolliver bent over the periscope again. "All right, Jake, I just thought you'd like to take a look."

Stock glanced around at the other men in the conning tower. When his eyes met those of Wes Clayton, he flushed slightly and looked away. He has the ability, Clayton thought, to look out of place wherever he is.

Without another word, Stock dropped down the ladder and out of sight. Now Clayton had the field to himself again. "How about that train, Captain?" It seemed a safe question.

But Tolliver did not reply, raptly intent again on what he saw through the exposed eye of the periscope. Only when the submarine's depth control went suddenly awry, dropping the periscope's eye beneath the surface, did he speak.

"Get me up!"

Hurried and profane orders were hurled to the diving station in the control room just below the conning tower, and the situation was remedied. Tolliver's eye never left the periscope. He continued to swing it slowly to the left, tracking with the train until it was completely out of sight. Then he stepped back and stood erect as he snapped the training handles up alongside the periscope shaft.

"Down scope!"

The shaft of the periscope, glistening with oil and

water, moved rapidly downward as it was lowered into the well by the electric motor. Standing alone, Jonathan Tolliver gave the impression of being rather tall. Actually he was slightly under six feet. At the age of forty-one, he was a man honed to razor sharpness by the war in which he had been an active participant for nearly four years. There was nothing wasted on Tolliver—no ounce of flesh, no pulse beat, no fleeting thought of the night or day. He was making his ninth war patrol as Commanding Officer of a combat submarine—his fourth with the *Mudskipper*. Two Navy Crosses and half a dozen lesser citations attested to his record during those nine patrols. The shattered remains of twenty-three Japanese ships—more than one hundred thousand tons of shipping—lay rusting on the bottom of the sea as mute and ghastly evidence of Tolliver's skill as a hunter and a killer.

Now he responded to Clayton's question as though it had just been asked. "Like a toy. It looked like a toy train."

Clayton was relieved to know that Tolliver had not really been as serious as he had appeared. "You're right, Captain. I didn't think of it at the time, but now that you mention it, it reminded me of the electric train I got when I was a kid—when I was about nine years old, I guess. Boy, it was a dandy—puffed real smoke out of the stack and everything." He was instantly lost in the memory, being a man who possessed the sort of uncomplicated mind which could range freely between past and present without being confused by the imponderables of the future.

"Boy, that was the best Christmas I ever had. You had a train like that when you were a kid too, I'll bet, Captain. I guess every kid . . ."

Tolliver's voice was flat and expressionless. "My brother

had a train when he was nine."

Clayton chuckled, happily recapturing and relishing his own memories. "I never had as much fun with anything as I had with that fool train. My Dad and I set it up down in the basement, the whole works, and I used to stay down there for hours playing with it—that is, when I could get my Dad to give it up. I still have most of it stored away somewhere . . ."

"What's the time?" Tolliver wore a watch on his own wrist, but it did not occur to him to check that.

"Oh nine eleven, Captain."

"You first sighted the train about ten minutes ago?"

Clayton nodded. "Something like that, I suppose."

"That means it probably reached our vicinity at approximately oh nine hundred."

"Yes sir. Why . . ."

"Be sure you enter that in the log, Wes—with the time."

Clayton grinned as he moved over to the plotting table where the *Mudskipper*'s logbook was stored. "You thinking about catching that train some morning, Captain?"

Tolliver did not reply. Instead, he turned to the duty officer, Lieutenant Tom Friday. "You have the con again, Tom. Resume the normal search pattern. I'll be in my quarters."

"Aye, aye, Captain." Friday was the submarine's Engineering Officer, an awkward-looking man whose huge hands always seemed to be flapping at his sides. Only when those hands touched some troublesome piece of machinery did they acquire grace and purpose.

"Any idea how long we're going to stay on this station, Captain?" he asked. "We haven't seen so much as a sampan since we got here."

The anger which, in recent days, had never been far

from the surface flared briefly in Tolliver's deep-set, startlingly green eyes. It was quickly brought under control. Tolliver knew anger for what it was, a weakness which was not to be displayed. "We'll be here until we are ordered out." It was a proper response, one which demonstrated a respect for the established order of things—for the chain of command, for the book, for the wisdom of his superiors. It was the correct response to give Tom Friday. Actually, Jonathan Tolliver felt little respect for any of these things.

He swung easily down the ladder to the control room where the men on watch were concerned with controlling the depth of the submerged *Mudskipper*. The duty officer there was a pink and pleasant faced Lieutenant junior grade named Bill Glasser, a man inevitably identified by the crew as "Pinkie." This was Glasser's first patrol under Tolliver, and he made the mistake of greeting his C.O. cheerfully.

"You got something up there, Captain?"

Tolliver turned and regarded Glasser in icy silence for a moment.

"Have you checked your trim since the morning dive, Mr. Glasser?"

"Yes, sir. First thing when I came on . . ."

"Then perhaps you can explain why you dunked the periscope on me a minute ago."

He spoke with a deceptive gentleness, and Glasser fell into the trap.

"Sorry about that, Captain. Guess we got a little careless for a minute and . . ."

The voice was still quiet, but the gentleness was replaced by cold steel. "Do you have any idea what could happen if you did that while I was making an approach

13

on a target, Mr. Glasser?"

Too late, Glasser realized his predicament, and his naturally pink face turned several shades darker. "Y-Yes, sir . . ."

"It could mean losing the target, Mr. Glasser, and it could also mean losing this submarine."

"I'll check the trim again, Captain . . ."

"You do that, Mr. Glasser."

Tolliver turned and ducked through the watertight door which led to the forward passageway before Glasser could say anything further. For several seconds a strained and awkward silence hung over the Control Room. Then Bill Glasser, his voice shrill with embarrassment, turned on the enlisted men at the manifold.

"Okay, let's get on the ball! Pump from number one auxiliary to number four!"

Henry Jackson—thin, balding—a Yeoman striker, had just happened to be in the control room during the incident. He was not on watch but had stopped by to shoot the breeze with another sailor. Now he left the control room and headed for his quarters in the *Mudskipper's* after torpedo room. Jackson was a born gossip, and the prospect of telling the men in the after room about Glasser's humiliation filled him with pleasure.

He was disappointed to find most of the off-duty section gathered around and giving their attention to a chess game between Signalman First Class Freddie Baldwin and Chief Torpedoman Amos Kenestrick. Jackson, wanting a totally attentive audience, edged into the circle of spectators and awaited his opportunity.

The two contestants sat on the edges of bunks facing each other across a battered chess board which rested on an improvised table. The bunks themselves were nestled

14

in among racks of torpedoes on either side of the compartment.

Baldwin, a husky, tow-headed man of twenty-two from Baltimore, wore only a pair of dungarees which had been cut off at the knees to convert them into shorts. In high school he had been a fullback on a team from the Baltimore Polytechnic Institute which had won the city championship for four straight years. The war had taken the place of college for him, and one of his constant fears was that the football scholarship to the University of Maryland which had been his for the taking would no longer be available after the war. Now his jutting chin rested on his hands as he hunched forward, studying his next move. His king was in deadly peril, and he knew it. Kenestrick, who was not as good a player as Baldwin, had suckered him into a foolish sacrifice of his knight on the previous move, and Baldwin was still seething with anger at himself for having been such a damned fool. He might use his castle to . . .

Jackson was tired of waiting. "Jeez, you guys should've heard the old man chewing out Pinkie Glasser a minute ago . . ."

Freddie Baldwin's battered face twisted in annoyance. "Knock it off, Jackson."

His opponent, Amos Kenestrick, laughed softly. He was a wiry, swarthy man of twenty-six, a veteran of four war patrols on the *Mudskipper*, and he knew he had Baldwin exactly where he wanted him. Three more moves, he told himself, just three . . .

"Don't pay no mind to him, Henry," he said. "What happened?"

That was all the encouragement Jackson needed. "Well, the old man must've been bugged about something, and

Pinkie made the fatal mistake of dunking the scope while the old man was taking a look at some damn thing or other. Then, when the old man came through Control, Pinkie opened his big fat mouth and said something cheerful, and that really tore it." Being an accomplished gossip, Jackson managed to expand the facts in order to make a better story for his audience. "You know the way the old man can chew out a guy—quiet as you please, but just like a damned meat grinder. He worked Pinkie over for about five minutes, and when he got through old Pinkie looked like he'd been run over by a truck."

Someone laughed. "Pinkie don't know the facts of life yet. I was with the skipper once when we'd had a long dry spell like this. Man, nobody cracks a smile when that happens. I'd as soon laugh at my mother's funeral."

"Are you guys gonna shut up?" Baldwin snarled. "How the hell can I concentrate with you flapping your gums?"

Kenestrick grinned maliciously. "It takes brains to concentrate, Baldwin. Just make your move, kid. It don't make any difference. You're a dead duck anyhow."

Baldwin glared at his opponent. He was not an easy loser. "I'll make my move when I'm damned good and ready."

The chess game was no longer the center of interest. A torpedoman striker, making his first patrol on the *Mudskipper*, called down from his bunk where he was stretched out on his stomach. "Hey, Chief, you were with the Captain when he knocked off those two tin cans in one day, weren't you?"

Kenestrick nodded importantly. "Yeah, that's the one he got his first Navy Cross for. It was the first run I made with him—down in the South China Sea. Man, that was a patrol!" He shot a glance at Freddie Baldwin and was pleased to note that his opponent was growing more and more irritated.

"I was on fire control, see, up in the conning tower, so I was right there where I could watch the old man. We'd been at general quarters all night, tracking this damned Jap convoy, and just when it started to get light, the old man started to make a run on this big tanker. He knew there were a couple of cans up there, but he never gave a good hoot in hell for them. He put three fish in that tanker, and while she was breaking up, this can started in after us. Nine out of ten guys would've turned tail, but the old man just pointed our stern at that can and waited—cool as you please—until she was inside of five hundred yards. Then he put two fish right down her gullet. Jeez, you should've heard when they hit . . ."

"All right, Kenestrick," Baldwin snarled. "You gonna play chess or tell war stories?"

"I'm waiting for you to make your move, kid. Now, like I was saying . . ."

Flushing angrily, Baldwin moved his castle to block Kenestrick's approach to his king—but only temporarily.

A quick glance at the board told Kenestrick that his estimate of three moves had been diminished by two. With a casual movement of his hand, the castle was captured by Kenestrick's queen which had been the width of the board away and unnoticed by Baldwin.

"Check," Kenestrick said cheerfully, then added, "Mate." With that he looked back up at the boy to whom he had been speaking. "We were still reloading the forward tubes when this other can started in, but the old man . . ."

"You lucky, big-mouthed . . ." Baldwin swept the remaining chessmen from the board and stood up, glaring at Kenestrick.

17

The chief was on his feet instantly, still grinning, but his eyes were hard and eager. "Watch it, kid."

"You watch it, you dirty . . ."

The chess board was knocked to the deck as Kenestrick lunged at Baldwin, swinging wildly, and, as though at a given signal, the watching men became a part of the melee—without purpose or cause. It was a fight, and that was enough for them. Henry Jackson, who loved to watch fights but was opposed to taking part in them, found himself grappling with a sailor named Esposito who was considerably smaller than Jackson. In desperation, Jackson swung a wild right and was surprised and pleased when it landed flush on the smaller man's mouth, bringing a trickle of blood. His pleasure was immediately put to rout by the fierce onslaught of Esposito which sent the two of them sprawling to the deck.

"Hold it! Dammit, *knock it off!*"

Jackson got away from his opponent and slid under a bunk gratefully as the big man in officer's khakis lunged into the brawling sailors, flinging men in all directions. As quickly as it had begun, the fight was ended, although several of the men, Kenestrick and Baldwin in particular, stood ready to go at it again.

Jake Stock stood between those two men, keenly aware of the hostility of the men around him. He had served with many of these men as a Chief Petty Officer. This was his first patrol as a commissioned officer. That commission was a source of tremendous pride to Jake Stock, but it was not a thing with which he had learned to feel at home.

As he stood now, looking at the angry faces all around him, he thought, as a Chief, I would have had no trouble with something like this. I was the youngest Chief on the boat, but I had the crew's respect. Now I've lost that.

Then, it would have simply been a question of knocking a few heads together. But as an officer, I can't do that.

He felt awkward and ill at ease, but his face did not betray this. Jake Stock's face was like the rest of the man—big and tough and powerful. There was not a man in the compartment he could not lick, and they all knew it. Instinctively he knew that this was the reason they obeyed him. He would have preferred other reasons, but he was stuck with their fear of him. It was not what he wanted, but he was able to settle for it.

"All right, who started this?"

Amos Kenestrick wiped a smear of blood from his lips. He and Jake Stock had been Chief Petty Officers together prior to Stock's commission, and he disliked the other man on a number of counts, not the least among them being the fact that Stock had achieved something which he, Kenestrick, would probably never achieve. It was a dislike which was intensified by the fact that the two men had once been close friends.

"Nobody started it, *sir*."

The emphasis was deliberate and unmistakable. Stock glared at him, his own sense of frustration compounded by the loneliness he felt at the loss of a friend. He was not a man who made or lost friends easily.

"Okay, Kenestrick, you're in charge of this compartment. I want a field day in here, starting as of now. I want this compartment ready for inspection in exactly one hour, and I mean an *inspection*. You guys sit around on your duffs in here, and all you can find to do is start a brawl. Okay, I'm giving you something to do. Hop to it, Kenestrick. I'll be back in one hour."

He avoided the contempt in Kenestrick's eyes as he turned abruptly and left the compartment. He knew what had started the fight, but he was helpless to deal with that problem. Petty punishment like the inspection would only serve temporarily to redirect the men's feelings of frustration from the real cause to a more available and tangible object—Jake Stock. The roots of the real cause of the fight in the after room went much deeper, and this knowledge only served to reinforce Stock's feeling of inadequacy as an officer.

There was only one man on the *Mudskipper* who could do anything about that problem, and Jake Stock made up his mind as he moved forward through the maneuvering and engine rooms of the submarine that he would take the problem directly to that man—to Jonathan Tolliver.

Following his dressing down of Bill Glasser, the *Mudskipper*'s Commanding Officer had gone to his own stateroom. There he had drawn the heavy curtains closing off the stateroom from the passageway and seated himself at his desk.

For a long time he merely sat there, unmoving, his face devoid of expression. Then he reached into a compartment in the top of the desk and took out a leather-bound patrol report book. He spent several minutes thumbing through the entries in it which gave a daily record of the *Mudskipper*'s activities since leaving her last refit at Midway. Ordinarily Tolliver enjoyed reading his own patrol reports. He had a way with words, and some of his fellow Commanding Officers had told him that they found a Tolliver Patrol Record better reading than fiction. The entries for this patrol, though, defied his talents . . .

He closed his eyes, wondering why he felt so drained and tense. A small muscle in the left side of his face twitched suddenly, and he forced himself to think about the report.

Perhaps only something he could create out of his own imagination would save this report from being a succession of dull and routine daily records—of dreary hours of waiting for an enemy who never appeared—of watching the fuel tanks empty while torpedoes remained unfired in their racks—of the gnawing, stretching tension fed by futility . . .

Only the sighting of the train would vary this day's entry. *Only the sighting of the train . . .*

Tolliver allowed himself to think about the train, and as he thought he reached into one of the drawers of his desk and took out several wooden match boxes. Idly, his hands apparently working independently of his mind, he began arranging those match boxes in a line across the metal surface of his desk—carefully butting each box against the next until they were strung out in a connected line—like the cars, he thought, of a train . . .

He sat studying them, his fingers drumming lightly on the edge of the desk, the muscle in his face jerking spasmodically, his face a study in concentration.

He could almost see the train—he *could* see it—crawling past the make-believe landscape, framed at first in the eye of the periscope and then, somehow, changed—running crazily around the track which formed a great ellipse on the cement floor of the basement—running past imitation trees and rocks, across the miniature bridge, past tiny houses and barns, disappearing into the cardboard tunnel, then emerging again. A boy was bent over the track, his hand on the control switch—first speeding, then slowing the train.

These things he saw through the eyes of another and smaller boy who was six-year-old Jonathan Tolliver—

hiding in the shadows and watching his older brother, David, playing with the electric train David had received for Christmas. It was David's train, not Jonathan's. Jonathan, their parents had said, was not yet old enough to have a train, and David Tolliver had said that his younger brother might watch him play with the train but that he must never touch it.

And so he watched, and as he watched the train became a hated thing, picking up speed as it moved jerkily around the track—became a blurred object of hate and jealousy until, suddenly, the younger boy was running toward it and kicking at the train, then pounding it with his tiny fists, flinging the toy engine and cars in all directions, screaming his hate . . .

Tolliver's fists smashed down on the line of match boxes, crushing them with blow after blow until nothing remained but the splintered ruins and scattered matches spread over the desk top like so many dead and broken bodies. Finally he stopped, raising his still-clenched fists to regard them with wonder. A tiny trickle of blood appeared on the knuckle of his right hand, and he put it to his mouth, sucking at it until it was clean.

After that he relaxed, a faint smile playing on his lips as he swept the mess from his desk and into the waste basket. Overt violence was a luxury which Tolliver seldom permitted himself, but this time it had served his purpose. It had confirmed something for him and turned a vague notion into a concrete plan.

"Captain . . ."

Tolliver started, checked the desk top again to make certain it was clear, and then answered, "What is it?"

The curtains were pulled aside to reveal the huge bulk

of Jake Stock.

"Come on in, Jake."

"You have a minute, Captain?"

"Sure."

Tolliver indicated his bunk, and Stock sat down heavily. In the tiny stateroom his size was exaggerated, and he looked out of place and cumbersome.

"What's on your mind, Jake?"

The big man scowled and cleared his throat. When he had served under Tolliver as an enlisted man, he had usually felt completely at ease with his C.O., but he had not yet been able to come to grips with himself as Tolliver's fellow officer.

"Well—it's about the crew, Captain."

"What about them?"

"I was just back in the after room. I had to break up a real free-for-all back there."

Tolliver's eyes narrowed. "A fight?"

I guess you'd call it that, but I think it was more than just a fight. It was more of a . . ." He strained for the right words. "More like letting off steam, I think. It's been building with these guys. They've been expecting something, I guess, and . . ."

"And they're not getting it?" Tolliver murmured, almost to himself.

Stock nodded. "That's about the size of it, Captain."

Tolliver nodded thoughtfully. "What is it they expect and aren't getting, Jake?"

"Hell, I don't know, Captain." Stock stirred uneasily. "I guess they figured they'd—I mean, they thought . . ."

Tolliver stopped him. "I can tell you what they expected. They expected the *Mudskipper* would be a boat they'd see some action on. Isn't that it?"

"I guess that's it, Captain."

"And they had every reason to expect just that," Tolliver said. "Because I expected the same thing. Listen, Jake, you've been with me now for . . . how many patrols?"

"Five . . . six counting this one."

"By all means, let's count this one. This one is very much to the point. Six patrols. I should think you'd know me rather well."

Stock shrugged. "Maybe . . ."

"Yes, you know me all right, Jake. Now what kind of a Commanding Officer am I?"

"A good one, Captain—the best . . ."

Tolliver's laugh was strained. "How good I am is not the point here, Jake. Neither of us is in a position to judge that—not yet. We lack the proper historical perspective. Good or not, I am a combat officer. A considerable sum of the taxpayers' money was spent to train me to do a job—to seek out the enemy and destroy him."

He reminds me of a schoolteacher, Stock thought. To look at him, you'd think he wasn't involved in this at all.

But Jake Stock knew Tolliver better than to believe he was not involved, and deeply. He had seen him like this before, and the calm, detached, objective air was a façade which concealed frighteningly fierce emotions. On a few occasions Jake Stock had seen that naked fury revealed, and he was not likely to forget those times.

Once, on the third patrol he had made with Tolliver, he had seen the C.O. turn on an unfortunate Ensign who had relayed an order incorrectly during an attack on a Japanese freighter. As a result of the young officer's error, the freighter had escaped, and for a moment it had seemed

24

that Tolliver would actually strike the other man. As it was he had lashed him with words so viciously that the Ensign had been reduced to a quivering wreck. Then the storm had passed, and as suddenly as he had lost control, Tolliver had been calm and dispassionate. It was not a thing to forget.

"Seek out and destroy," Tolliver was saying again. "That's what I was trained to do—not to sit around and wait until my fuel tanks are empty so I can go crawling back with my tail between my legs and all my torpedoes still in their racks. That has never happened to me, Jake, and the crew knows it. So, if they are growing restless, I can understand their feelings, because I am growing restless too."

"I guess you're right, Captain, but what can we do? We're stuck with this area—for a while at least . . ."

"Not just for a while, Jake—for the rest of this patrol."

"Well," Stock said, "if that's the case, I was just wondering if there isn't some way we could get the crew to—well, accept things the way they are. If you could talk to them . . ."

"No!" Tolliver broke in sharply. "I don't want them to accept it any more than I do." He shook his head slowly, passing the back of his hand over his eyes as though to clear them. Then he looked at Stock. "How about you, Jake? Do you accept it?"

Stock was puzzled and disturbed. He had never seen Tolliver like this. The man looked drawn and gray suddenly, as though a mountainous fatigue had caught him without warning.

"Do you, Jake?" The question was almost a threat.

"I'm not sure what you mean, Captain. It's just the way

things are, that's all."

Tolliver's face cleared, and he smiled as he continued to look at the big man. He was aware of the agonizing fatigue which had gripped him, but he had fought it off. He was still his own master. He concentrated on Jake Stock, liking the man because he was a thing which Jonathan Tolliver had created. He had taken the raw material of a young Chief Petty Officer and shaped and formed it into an officer and a gentleman. Now Jake Stock was his creature, a valuable cog in the fighting machine which Tolliver controlled with *his* brain and *his* daring.

"And you can sit there and say it doesn't bother you?" he asked. Then, abruptly, he threw back his head and laughed—in a new mood, like a boy, eager to share a new thought with a friend. "Come on, Jake, I know better. We've been through a few things together, you and I. I've seen you in action, Jake—and when the going gets hard, that's when you are at your best. Remember when we were in the Formosa Strait?"

"Sure, Captain."

"You were still a Chief then." Tolliver did not want to lose an opportunity to remind Stock of his status.

"Yes, sir."

Tolliver leaned back in his chair and slapped his hands together in the sheer joy of the memory. "By all that's holy, Jake, I never saw a setup like that in my life. There were at least a dozen ships anchored in that harbor—just riding there at anchor—overlapping targets! It was something you dream about—pray for, and you never get it, but there it was—*real!* The only thing I had to worry about was not wasting too many torpedoes on one ship. You remember that?"

Stock nodded heavily. He remembered. He had been at

Tolliver's side that morning. He had been a part of the machine, and he had known the excitement—but despite all this, he knew that the quality of his memory did not match that of Tolliver's. The chasm between them extended to recollections of the past as well as to the realities of the present.

Now Tolliver's voice took on a soft, almost dreamlike quality as he continued. "Six of them, Jake—that's the score I made that morning—six ships. And it was so easy. I watched six of them go down in one attack, and we damaged at least three more. One day's work . . ."

"Yes, sir."

"They gave me my second Navy Cross for that day's work, Jake."

"Yes, sir. I remember."

"But that is not the important point, Jake." Tolliver leaned forward, intent on making his point, a teacher anxious to drive home the significant portion of his lecture. "The Navy Crosses mean nothing to me, Jake, but what I did does have meaning, because *that is what I was trained to do*. It cost a considerable amount of money to produce a man like me, and it is my duty to pay off that investment in the only way I can."

Jake Stock had seen Tolliver in this mood before, and, as always, he found himself not only puzzled but vaguely frightened by the quiet and deadly intensity of the man. It was an intensity which projected itself as a force, affecting anyone it touched and making him its victim, willing or otherwise. Stock was also capable of anger, but with him it usually took the form of a spontaneous emotion, one which erupted when he could no longer contain some frustration. Normally, he tended to be withdrawn and placid—even gentle, although he would never have so described himself. He knew his own great physical strength, and he had lived for nearly four years in the violent context of war—so that the gentleness which was an essential part of his nature was virtually unknown to him. And the thing which he recognized in Tolliver which he himself had never possessed was the ability to affect others, to infect them with his own ideas and emotions and drives.

Now he tried to offset Tolliver's intensity with a grin which did not quite materialize. "You've given them their money's worth, Captain. If any man has . . ."

"They never get their money's worth. You have to keep on, as long as there is an enemy to kill, you must keep on killing him. There are no quotas out here, Jake. It's not like going hunting and bagging your limit and then having to stop. There is no limit here. You can shoot as much as you can find." He leaned back in his chair, his eyes almost closed, and Stock had the uncomfortable feeling of watching the man struggle with an agony which should be completely private. "The war is almost over, Jake. Did you know that?"

"It figures, Captain. If what we hear about the way our bombers are clobbering Japan is true, then I don't see how they can hold out much longer."

Tolliver nodded wearily, his body sagging. "It's true all right. I've seen intelligence reports. Maybe a couple of months—maybe less. This could be the last patrol I'll make in this one . . ." His voice trailed off, and the two men sat sharing a strained silence.

Finally Stock stirred and cleared his throat. "I'd better shove off, Captain. I just thought you ought to know about what happened."

Tolliver did not look up. He was lost in thoughts which did not include Jake Stock. "Yes. Thanks, Jake."

At the curtained partition, Stock hesitated. "Captain, I was just thinking—maybe if the crew could be made to understand—I mean about the war being almost over—it might calm them down a little."

Tolliver shook his head. "No. I don't want them calmed down. I know what their problem is, and it's my duty to take care of it. They want action . . ."

"But it looks like all the Jap shipping is gone—at least in these waters."

Unexpectedly, Tolliver was smiling. "Yes, Jake, I daresay you're right."

"Then," Stock spread his hands helplessly, "I don't understand . . ."

"Don't worry about it, Jake. You will."

It's no use, Stock thought. I've stuck my neck out far enough already. That was a thing he remembered from his long years as an enlisted man. Don't stick your neck out. Let someone else do the thinking. He nodded and said, "Yes, sir." And he turned to leave the stateroom, but Tolliver stopped him again.

"Jake . . ."

He turned back. "Yes, sir?"

"I'm curious about one thing. How do you feel about all this? I mean, we both have a fairly good idea how the crew feels, and I've been frank with you about my feelings. How do you like sitting out here and waiting for the war to end without firing a single torpedo?"

The question took Stock by surprise, and he did not answer immediately. He realized that his initial impulse was to give Tolliver the answer he wanted to hear, but he could not obey that impulse.

"I'm not sure, Captain," he said finally. "I've been on combat duty most of the war—for almost four years . . ."

Now he chose his words with care. "I—I think I'd be just as happy to see it over and done with."

Tolliver studied him for a moment, a slight smile playing on his lips. "In other words, if the war ended today—with us sitting here, doing nothing—you'd be satisfied?"

It was a loaded question, and Jake Stock knew it. He sensed further that in some strange way he had reached a critical point in his long relationship with the man he had come to regard as a virtual god. It was a painful realization, but there was no way of avoiding it. Stock was a simple man, but he was also an honest one.

He looked Tolliver straight in the eye, not an easy task for him under the circumstances, and he said, "Yes, sir. I'd be a lot more than just satisfied. I'd be happy as hell."

It was Tolliver whose eyes broke away first. He glanced down at his desk, and his voice was remote. "That's very interesting, Jake. Close those curtains on the way out, will you?"

When Stock had gone, Jonathan Tolliver remained seated for a long time, unmoving, his eyes half closed. An observer would have thought him to be devoid of life or thought—but his thoughts were active and dealt with both life and death. Finally he stirred himself and left his quarters in the direction of the control room. As he entered that compartment, Bill Glasser shot an uneasy glance at him and desperately checked the submarine's trim bubble.

Tolliver walked over to stand beside the junior officer.

"Got her steady now, Bill?"

"I think so, Captain . . ."

"Good boy!" He clapped Glasser lightly on the shoulder, and the diving officer glowed. "She looks steady as a rock, Bill."

And, as the *Mudskipper's* skipper climbed the ladder to the conning tower, he left behind him a man who knew, in that golden moment, the wonder of having been found pleasing in the eyes of a god.

Two

⚓

THE BOY'S NAME was Takeo. He was nine years old, and he lived with his mother and his grandfather on a small farm which was located about two miles from the railroad tracks. Takeo's father had gone away to serve in the Imperial Navy at the beginning of the war. Takeo had been only five years old then, and his memories of his father were based on things his mother had told him and on the photograph which occupied the place of honor in the shrine on the wall of the one-room wooden shack which was Takeo's home. That photograph had been made when Takeo's father was a very young man, just after he had married Takeo's mother.

His father had been more of a fisherman than a farmer, and he had gone out to sea with other men from the region when the salmon and tunny were running. Most of the stories told Takeo by his mother had to do with the fishing—stories his father had brought home from long days and nights at sea. Then, when the war with the hated Americans had come, Takeo's father had left his home and his family, and he had never returned—not even for one final visit. The big ship on which he had served had been destroyed by a submarine, and Takeo's father had died, fighting for his Emperor whom he had never seen and for his homeland of which he had seen only a very little. Now all that remained of him was the little shrine and the faded photograph and a wooden box of ragged clothing and the stories. And, of course, Takeo—who was flesh of his father's flesh—Takeo remained to take his father's place.

Now Takeo and his mother's father worked on the farm for long, back-breaking days to raise enough food to sustain them. The grandfather was very old, and he seldom spoke and never smiled. He worked as much as he was able, and the remainder of the time he sat on a cushion on the floor or outside in the sun and smoked his pipe and stared straight ahead and ate his tiny portion of rice and soy beans and slept. There were a few other boys on nearby farms, but, they, like Takeo, had to work most of the time, and he seldom saw any of them. He knew that one day, when the war was over and the Americans had been destroyed, he would grow to be a man like his father, and when that happened he would go away from the farm to do a man's work. It would not be as a fisherman. He hated the sea, because the sea and the Americans had taken his father from him. There was other work for a man to do.

He reached the rock early this morning. The train was not yet in sight, but he climbed the rock anyhow and waited, his eyes turned in the direction of Nemuro. Once his mother had taken him to Nemuro. It was a very large place with many buildings and shops and crowds of people. The train came from Nemuro, he knew, and it went on to a place he had never been, a great city which was called Kushiro. Kushiro, he had heard, was much larger even than Nemuro, although this was difficult to believe. And every morning the train came from Nemuro on its way to Kushiro.

He could see it in the distance, see its smoke first and finally the mighty locomotive itself, looking quite small at first, but growing larger and larger as it drew near. Soon it would be making its turn, and very solemnly, but with a joy and a wonder which his face did not reveal, Takeo raised his right hand. He knew that the man who rode in the locomotive would see him, and that someday he might raise his own hand to return Takeo's greeting. The train was almost upon him now, and he saw the man who ran the train. The man saw him, and Takeo was sure that the man recognized him, even though he gave no sign. As the train rumbled by, the boy turned so that his eyes remained fixed on that shining locomotive.

That was the work Takeo would do when he was a man. He would wear a cap and fine gloves, and he would sit at the wonderful machine which made the train run, and he would send his train thundering along between two great cities.

He stood atop the rock and watched until the train was out of sight. Then he lowered his hand and started walking very slowly back in the direction of his home. There was much work to be done that day, and he knew that his mother and grandfather would already be in the fields and that they would scold him and call him lazy because he was late. But he did not mind. His thoughts were filled with the locomotive and the man who ran the locomotive. And then, a strange thought struck him—for the first time really. If the train went from Nemuro to Kushiro each morning, then, at some time the train must also return from Kushiro to Nemuro. From the fields where he worked, he could not see the train but he was sure he could hear it and, perhaps, see the smoke from its stack— but he had never seen or heard it except in the mornings when it was always going in the same direction. The train must return at night when Takeo was asleep. He tried to imagine what the train would look like at night. He knew that there was fire inside the locomotive, and perhaps at night that fire would actually belch forth, showing red and fierce like a dragon. If he stood on the rock at night, with his hand raised, would the man inside the locomotive be able to see him?

These things, Takeo wondered about and took with him to the fields, and, as he worked, he decided that one night, one night very soon, he would go out and discover the answers for himself.

"There she blows!"

Tolliver's voice was buoyant. With a quick, practiced motion his right hand twisted the periscope's focusing handle.

"What's the time, Wes?"

"Oh nine two, Captain." The Executive Officer was standing beside him.

"Looks like they run a pretty good schedule, doesn't it? How far is that off yesterday's time?"

"Not more than a couple of minutes."

"Record this time in the log and compare them, Wes."

"You sound like you're getting downright fond of that Jap train, Captain." Clayton chuckled. He was feeling good because Tolliver's mood had so obviously taken an upward turn. Indeed, the entire crew seemed to have brightened during the past day, as though they were somehow infected by their Commanding Officer. Wes Clayton did not pretend to understand the change in Tolliver. He was content that it had taken place, and only vaguely did he sense that the Japanese train was somehow a part of it. Who knows, he thought, maybe the old man just gets a boot out of watching trains. Whatever it was, Clayton was grateful for it. It made life a lot more pleasant aboard the *Mudskipper.*

Tolliver was still intent on following the train's progress through the periscope. "Yes, Wes, I think I am growing very fond of that train." He straightened. "Down scope." His smile was thoughtful and detached. "Looks like we ought to be able to count on its reaching our position here within a few minutes either way of oh nine hundred, right?"

Clayton had moved over to check the previous day's entry in the log. "Looks that way, Captain. Of course, we've only seen it a couple of times . . ."

"Good!" Tolliver slapped his hands together briskly. "Wes, I'll want to see you and Jake Stock in the wardroom right away. Find him and bring him along."

"Aye, aye, Captain." Clayton dropped out of sight down the ladder to the control room.

Tolliver turned to Tom Friday. "All right, Tom, she's all yours. Resume the normal patrol routine, but keep a particularly sharp eye out along the coast. Anything you see that's out of the ordinary, make a note of it—any other trains—any vehicular traffic at all. Right?"

"Yes, sir."

"Also, I want you to be more than usually alert for any aircraft in the area. Every time you make a surface sweep, check for aircraft and make a record of any you see along with the time, and the apparent direction of flight."

With that, Tolliver lowered himself down to the control room. He nudged Bill Glasser good-naturedly in the ribs and exchanged quips with the two sailors on the diving plane controls before moving on forward to the wardroom. In the tiny galley adjoining the officer's wardroom, Steward's Mate First Class Roy Watson was just finishing his own breakfast. When he heard Tolliver, he opened the sliding windows which provided access between the galley and the serving counter in the wardroom and put his head through. "You ready for some breakfast now, Captain?"

Roy Watson had served with Tolliver for six war patrols, and his relationship with his C.O. was governed almost entirely by intuition. It was Watson's boast that he knew what Tolliver wanted before Tolliver himself knew, and on this morning he had already planned a breakfast menu consisting of fruit juice, French toast, ham, and hash browned potatoes. He was properly shocked when Tolliver indicated that he had no interest in breakfast.

"Got everything all ready to go, Captain. It wouldn't take no time at all . . ."

"Not now, Roy, but I would like a pot of fresh coffee and three mugs, on the double."

Watson shook his head resentfully. "Yes, sir. Got a fresh pot just done."

"Good. Then I want you to clear out for a while, Roy. I'll want privacy in here and plenty of it."

This was the final insult. Watson stalked into the wardroom, placed the coffee on the table with patently wounded dignity, and departed.

A few minutes later, with the curtains drawn sealing off

the wardroom, Tolliver, the Executive Officer, and Jake Stock were seated at the table. Before them on the green billiard cloth table cover were three steaming mugs of coffee. Wes Clayton was puffing on a battered corncob pipe, a gift from his wife who had told him it made him look like General MacArthur, a dubious asset to Clayton's Navy-orientated point of view. Nevertheless, he had grown very fond of the pipe. Jake Stock had just lighted a cigarette. Tolliver, who did not smoke, was drumming his fingers nervously on the table. Then, suddenly, he clapped his hands together in a characteristic gesture and smiled at the other two men.

"Wes—Jake—how would you evaluate our chances of destroying any of the enemy on this patrol?"

Clayton looked puzzled. "You mean if we stay in this area, Captain?"

"That's precisely what I mean."

The *Mudskipper's* Executive Officer had the uncomfortable feeling of having been asked a simple question which would somehow turn out to have a complicated answer, and he was not a man to be happy with complexities. However, he played it the only way he was capable of playing it. He gave Tolliver an honest answer.

"I'd say about the same chance as a snowball in a bonfire. We've got maybe one more week before we're going to have to head for the barn on account of fuel, and my guess is that the Japs have more shipping running down the main street of Tokyo than they have around here."

Tolliver nodded, apparently satisfied with the answer. "How about you, Jake?"

Stock glanced down at his huge hands for a moment before answering. He had not really talked with Tolliver since their conversation in the latter's stateroom the day before, but he was aware of the abrupt and inexplicable change in Tolliver's attitude. He had been cheerful—too damned cheerful, considering the way things were.

"Come on, Jake," Tolliver urged. "What's your opinion?"

"It's simple, Captain," Stock murmured finally. "If they're not up there, we can't sink them."

Tolliver leaned back with a chuckle. "Sink? Now who said anything about sinking anybody? I asked what our chances are of destroying any of the enemy. There are many ways of destroying the enemy, Jake. A bomber crew unloads its bombs over Tokyo—a sniper in some jungle takes aim and squeezes the trigger—all destroying the enemy, one way or the other. Different approaches to the same problem, but leading to the same result."

His expression changed in an instant, and he thrust himself forward, his face tight and hard. "And I say we are out here for that one reason—to destroy the enemy—whenever and however we can."

Neither of the other men spoke for a moment. Then Wes Clayton cleared his throat nervously and nodded. "I'm with you, Captain, but we haven't even smelled any shipping here, and—"

"Shipping! Who mentioned shipping? I have another kind of target in mind." Tolliver lifted his mug of coffee, drained it, and slapped it back on the table with a flourish. His audience was with him now, and he savored their rapt attention. "Come on, Wes, I'm surprised you haven't figured this one out for yourself by now. Why do you think I've made such a point of checking his schedule? Do you think I just derive some sort of strange pleasure from looking at trains?"

Clayton's reaction was quite satisfactory. "You—you mean, *that* train?"

Tolliver took a deep breath and inclined his head. "To the best of my knowledge, Wes, that's the only train around here."

"You're going to sink that train?"

Tolliver threw back his head and whooped with laughter. "By God, Wes, you are in a rut. Sink it? Sure, why not? We'll fire three torpedoes set for dry ground running and sink it. Come on, Wes, use your head!"

"But how . . ."

"Very simple. Look, we know its schedule, or we will in another two days. We haven't seen it making a return run, so that must be at night, and we should be able to nail that down pretty close. My guess is that the Japanese who runs that train is punctual to a fault. He doesn't know how to be late. We simply extend our normal method of operation. We will put a landing party ashore, and we will leave that train a little present placed with loving care right on the tracks. And when it is all over, we will send off a message to ComSubPac that reads, SIGHTED TRAIN. BLEW UP SAME." He laughed with obvious delight.

Wes Clayton was nodding, a broad grin spreading over his homely face. "Yeah, Captain! Why not? Why the hell not?"

Jake Stock had not spoken. Tolliver leaned toward him.

"How about it, Jake? Does that sound like good clean outdoors-type fun to you?"

Stock did not look up. "Yeah, Captain. I guess it could be done all right." But he felt no enthusiasm for the idea, and his voice made this clear. Tolliver frowned.

"What's troubling you, Jake?"

"There're—lots of angles, Captain." He spoke very slowly, anxious to say it the way he wanted and knowing it would not be easy. "We—well, we've never had any training for that kind of operation—a landing party and all, I mean. It takes a lot of . . . coordination and planning . . ."

"Don't evade the question, Jake. What's really bothering you?"

The blunt honesty which was a basic character trait of Jake Stock had trouble coming to the surface in the face of Tolliver's predictable disapproval.

"What I'm wondering, Captain, is—well, how important would it be if we did—I mean, really blow up that train . . ."

Tolliver's eyes narrowed, but there was no sign of the explosion Stock had feared. "Jake!" Actually the tone of voice was gentle and chiding rather than angry. "What sort of question is that? I thought I'd already explained it to you. It would be destruction of the enemy and his equipment—our reason for being here. The only reason we're here."

Stop it right here, Stock warned himself. There is not a thing you can say that will make sense to Tolliver. I'm not even sure that what I want to say makes any sense to me.

But he could not stop.

"I know that, Captain, but how important are the few Japs we might kill—and how important is that train? There's no industry up here. I'd guess it's mostly fishing ports . . ."

"And fish is food, right?" Tolliver's voice remained calm and patient. He might have been a teacher going over a problem with an unusually slow student, anxious to make his point and willing to take as much time as necessary to do so. "Since when is food unimportant to a war machine, Jake? Now, if we spotted a freighter, and we knew it was loaded with food, we'd sink it, wouldn't we?"

Stock nodded. "Yes, sir, but—"

"Now but me no buts!" A slight edge had crept into Tolliver's words now. "Come on, Jake, we've been through a few things together, and I've never known you to back away from anything. What is it this time? What makes this different?"

It was a question Stock had desperately been asking himself, and he had found no answer.

"Nothing, Captain. I guess I was just taken a little by surprise . . ."

Tolliver slapped his hands together and laughed. "If you think you were taken by surprise, try to picture how the engineer on that train will feel." He had brushed Stock's objections aside as though they had never existed. His own enthusiasm was now in full control. "We, Jake—I want this! This war is almost over, and it may be the only war I'll ever have. They've tried to turn it over to the bombers, and we're supposed to sit quietly and mind our manners until they've finished our war for us, so we can all go home and settle down with our pipes and our slippers and spend the remainder of our lives telling war stories to a bunch of youngsters who will be too busy with wars of their own to care about ours." He smiled—almost shyly, Stock noted. "Perhaps—perhaps, I only want one more story to tell them—a story about a train."

He sank back and stared reflectively at the other two men. Then he said quietly, "This may very well be the last run I'll make as the Commanding Officer of a combat submarine. I'm forty-one years old. That's not very old, you know. I'll probably live another thirty years or so. But the reason for my living may be gone in a week or two from now—and it may never come back again. You might call it pride, but I think it's a little more than that. At least, it is what Browning called a 'soldier's pride.' And that's a special breed of pride, gentlemen."

He paused, poured himself another cup of coffee, and then looked up with a grin. Jake Stock was startled by the way Tolliver's face could change. Suddenly he looked like a little boy, charming and mischievous.

"All right—there's more. I'll be completely honest with you. This is for me—a selfish thing I want for Jonathan Tolliver. I know you're thinking that, and you're right. The train is what I want, and the train is what I'm going to get. I'll tell you something—when I was a boy, I seldom got things I wanted. I was not a spoiled or pampered child. Now in some cases, that might result in a man who is resigned to not having his way, but it didn't work like that with me." His tone remained light, but neither Stock nor Clayton had any doubts about the complete seriousness of what he was saying.

"When I want something now, I mean to have it. And *I want that train*." He glanced from one man to the other, then looked directly at Jake Stock. "And you, Jake—you are going to get it for me."

"Okay, Captain." Jake Stock's voice was flat. "When?"

Wes Clayton broke in, "Look, Captain, I've got an idea. Why not—"

"Hold it, Wes!" Tolliver was not interested in any ideas his Exec might have. "You still don't like it, do you, Jake?"

"It's not important whether I like it or not, Captain . . ."

"No, it's not important, but I just want to know where we stand."

"All right." He tried to match Tolliver's stare and failed. "I'm not sure I like it, but I'll do my best."

Tolliver's teeth flashed in a wolfish grin. "Of course you will, Jake. That's why I want you to do this job." His hands slapped together sharply. "Now, let's get down to business. You'll need a package of explosives—big enough to do the job and portable enough to get ashore in the rubber boat, right?"

Stock nodded. "That's right, Captain."

"And you'll have to rig a detonator?"

"We can probably use one from a torpedo."

"Good! We have plenty of torpedoes to spare. Now how do you figure to set it off? Rig a time fuse?"

Stock thought for a moment. "It'd probably be better to use a microswitch. It could be placed right on the track, and when the train's wheels hit it—"

"Boom!" Wes Clayton laughed excitedly.

Stock stared at him, then nodded slowly. "That's right."

Tolliver ignored the Executive Officer. "How long would it take you to rig the bomb?"

"I'm not sure. With luck, maybe six, eight hours." Despite his reservations, Stock was beginning to feel the excitement growing in himself, and he was grateful for this. "I've never made a bomb before."

Tolliver laughed. "And no submarine has ever blown up a train before. It looks like a time for firsts. The bomb, Jake, how much do you figure it'll weigh?"

"I'm not sure, but my guess would be not much over fifty pounds, maybe less, but at least thirty pounds."

"Good enough. You'll want to pick a landing party to go along with you. How many men?"

This question gave Stock further pause. He had been mildly disturbed by the fact that he was going to have to risk his own neck on what seemed to him a foolish mission, but the fact that others would also be involved was something else.

44

"I don't know—maybe three."

"Three in addition to you?"

"Yes."

"You're sure that'll be enough?" Wes Clayton, determined not to be completely shut out of the planning, made the question somehow into a challenge.

Stock's grin was bleak. "Unless there's something or somebody ashore to argue with us, the fewer people we use the better."

Clayton was persistent. "My idea would be able to take more. I mean, there's no point in taking—"

"If Jake says three, then three it is," Tolliver broke in sharply. "You pick the three you want, Jake, and then get to work on the bomb. You'll want all three men thoroughly familiar with the bomb and the entire operation— just in case." Tolliver sat silently for a moment, his face a study in concentration. "Tonight, Jake, I think you ought to do a little reconnoitering. Take yourself some shore leave."

"You mean, go ashore tonight and check it out and then take the bomb in tomorrow?"

"Right."

It made sense, Stock thought—as much as anything about the whole crazy business made sense.

"Okay. I'll only need to take one man with me tonight."

"You pick your man. We'll surface as soon as it's dark. Wes, I'll want to get in as close to shore as we can go and as near the point where we've been observing the train as possible—ready to surface immediately when it is dark enough for safe cover. Get the rubber boat checked and have an air line rigged and ready to take topside to inflate it."

Wes Clayton beamed at having been finally brought

into things. Then he thought of something and looked worried again. "I hope we can find the damned thing."

"What?"

"That rubber boat. I mean, we've never had any use for it, and—"

Jake Stock broke in, "It's stored in the forward room, Wes. I know where it is."

Clayton breathed a sigh of relief. "Good. I thought it was probably there, but—"

"As Executive Officer," Tolliver said coldly, "you should damned well do more than think you know where an important piece of equipment is on this submarine."

Stock was acutely aware of the agony the rebuke brought Clayton, and he was equally aware of the fact that his own knowledge concerning the whereabouts of the rubber boat in the face of the Exec's obvious ignorance would do nothing to endear him to Clayton. It was another small wedge driven between them, adding to the already considerable gap which separated him from Clayton—a gap which likewise existed between him and all the officers on the *Mudskipper*—all but Tolliver. His relationship with Jonathan Tolliver was of a special order of disparity.

"Have you ever handled one of those boats, Jake?" Tolliver asked him.

"No, sir, but I don't think it'll be any trouble. You sit in it, and you paddle."

The *Mudskipper's* C.O. stared at him for a moment, then laughed. "That's what I like about you, Jake. You don't try to make simple things complicated."

Clayton stirred unhappily. "Captain, suppose I go locate that boat now, if I'm not needed for anything else here . . ."

Tolliver glanced at him. "Are you sure you can manage to find it, Wes?"

"Yes, sir." The Executive Officer's face was crimson.

"All right. Go ahead, then. There are a few more things I want to check out with Jake."

When the two men were alone in the wardroom, Tolliver sat for several minutes, drinking his coffee in silence. Watching him, Jake Stock was filled with a variety of emotions. He often thought of the other man the way he might have thought of his father—if he had ever known his father.

Jake Stock's father had died, trapped two hundred feet beneath the ground in a West Virginia coal mine, two months before his only son was born.

And Stock had known no father until Jonathan Tolliver had somehow filled that void in his life. He had not known how his father had died until he was seven years old, and then his mother had told him—of how she had stood through three long days and nights while rescuers tried in vain to reach the men who had been trapped below ground—of how they had finally told her it was hopeless, that the men were dead. And the boy had gone to his room and locked himself inside and cried until he was sick.

Jake Stock had not cried since that time.

"All right, Jake," Tolliver broke the long silence. "We're alone now, and if there's anything you want to say, now is the time."

"No, Captain. There's nothing. I was only wondering . . ."

"Why I'm so dead set on that train?"

Stock did not reply, but Tolliver nodded, smiling.

"Sure you are, and why not? It's a harebrained, wild

scheme, you're thinking, and under any other circumstances, you'd probably be right, Jake, but not with me—and you know that. Of all the men on this boat, I think you know me best. You've been through more with me than any of the others . . ."

He paused, and his eyes closed. Then, with a seeming effort, he opened them and blinked several times. Once again he seemed to have suddenly been enveloped in a giant gray fist of fatigue. His shoulders hunched forward as he continued to speak.

"D'you know how long it has been since I've had a leave, Jake? I don't mean the two weeks rest camp kind of leave we all take after a patrol. I mean a leave—to go home—to get away from the war. Do you know how long?"

"I guess it's been a long time, Captain. I mean, not since I've been with you."

Tolliver nodded. "You're right. This is the sixth patrol I've made without a break. I went back home just before that first run you made with me, but it was no good. There isn't any proper home for a man at war, Jake. The only home I have is here."

His face was tight and drawn, and his eyes seemed to have taken on a special kind of intensity as though they were struggling to keep the man in touch with the world around him.

"Nobody back there understands what it is out here, Jake. We're in two different worlds—those of us here and the people back in the States. I had nothing to say to them, and they had nothing to say to me. Even my wife . . . had nothing to say to me . . ."

It is not that way with Helen, Jake Stock thought, grasping at that truth and clinging to it desperately.

"In a way, Jake, I think I love the enemy with the love I would give my wife and my friends under ordinary circumstances. When I go after an enemy ship, when I see my torpedoes exploding against the side of an enemy ship, then I am expressing that love. There's a poem by Oscar Wilde that says the same thing. D'you read poetry, Jake?"

Once, when they had been sitting together out on the porch of their home, in the darkness of a summer night, Stock had found himself trying to say things to his wife, Helen—things he felt but had never been able to put into words. It had been the last time he was home on leave, and every moment together had been a precious thing. He struggled to find the right words, and, because it was dark, he was able somehow to continue until all the words had been said. And Helen—the miracle of warmth and love which was Helen—had turned to him and held his face in her small hands there in the darkness and called him a poet. And in the darkness, with the sweetness of their little time together upon him, he could believe her. This was Jake Stock's only exposure to poetry.

"Not very much, Captain."

"You should. Poets have a way of getting at the truth of things. This poem by Oscar Wilde—it goes like this:

> *And each man kills the thing he loves.*
> *By all let this be heard.*
> *The coward does it with a kiss,*
> *The brave man with a sword.*"

It was cool in the wardroom, but sweat stood out on Tolliver's forehead. "D'you understand what that means, Jake? The brave man kills the thing he loves—with a sword. There is no stronger force than love, Jake. No stronger force . . ."

He seemed to sag, the life draining out of him, and Jake Stock thought for an instant that he was going to collapse. Then he stirred, and a touch of the brightness returned to his eyes. "Perhaps that is the way I am with that train, Jake." He leaned forward, seeming almost to plead for understanding. "Perhaps, from the moment I saw that train, I loved it—and, loving it, I must destroy it. Do you understand that, Jake?"

Jake Stock's understanding filled him with a great pity and a sense of horror. But he was neither articulate nor subtle enough to answer Jonathan Tolliver. There might have been a time when he could simply have turned his back on Tolliver, but that time was past. Jake Stock had made his choice—to follow Tolliver wherever he might lead, and there was no turning back from that choice.

Because he knew what Tolliver was now—a man who had been stretched out on the wheel of war dangerously near the breaking point. For as long as Jake could remember in his relationship with Tolliver, it had been Jake Stock who needed Jonathan Tolliver. Now, the situation was reversed.

"You do understand, don't you, Jake?" It was a plea. Stock nodded slowly.

"Yes, Captain. I understand."

Three

⚓

THE OLD MAN's name was Kurita. He had accepted the position as leader of the coastal patrol group with pride, because it set him above his companions. It was Kurita who was permitted to carry the rifle, while the others had merely knives and sticks and pitchforks. It was Kurita who saw to it that the members of the patrol were present each evening to take up their station and to make periodic inspections of the ten-mile stretch of coastline. It was Kurita who had the important responsibility of turning in weekly reports to the officer who came through from Kushiro.

For more than three years, Kurita and his patrol had done their job faithfully. In those three years, Kurita had never had anything of interest or importance to report, and, in recent months, he had begun to lose his enthusiasm for the job. The barren stretch of coast along which the train tracks ran was always the same. The nights were long, and it was difficult for a man to get any decent rest out in the open. Kurita's bones were weary and aching, and his few remaining teeth bothered him dreadfully. He huddled under the partial shelter of the rock and stared into the blackness of the night which was still young. There was a shroud of fog settling around him, and this added to his gloom. Endless hours stretched ahead until it would be light, and he and his men would be able to return to their homes. There were times of late when Kurita had seriously considered calling the other men together and getting them to agree simply to stay at home during the long nights. Then, when the officer came through for his report, Kurita would meet him and report that nothing of any consequence had taken place. It would be the truth, and he and the other men would be spared those long, chilling nights in the open. But Kurita did not do this. Something within him—a fear perhaps, a sense of duty, an inability to lie—drove him to muster his patrol each evening and march them out to the coast where they remained until the sun rose the next morning.

And each night only one thing happened to break the dreadful monotony of darkness. The train, on its return from Kushiro, would rumble out of the darkness, sparks spewing from its stack. When this happened, Kurita and his men would stand and watch the train, deriving a bit of imaginary warmth from the great locomotive of steel and the fire which raged within its belly. Sometimes the men would shout greetings to the train in shrill, old men's voices which were lost in the noise of the wheels on the tracks and the pounding song of the locomotive itself. They would shout and wave their weary arms and watch until the train had been swallowed up again by the blackness. And then they would huddle together again or go trudging along the path to guard the shores of their land against an enemy none of them had ever seen—an enemy who had no reality for them.

They would see the train again the next morning as they made their way back to their homes, but by that time they would be too weary to shout or even look at the train. It was only in the lonely blackness of the night that the train held any meaning for Kurita and his men.

And now he sat, his ancient rifle clutched tightly in one hand, his eyes staring into the blackness and the fog, waiting for the train.

"Stand by to surface!"

In the faint red glow of the night lighting, the *Mudskipper*'s conning tower had a weird, other-world look. Jonathan Tolliver stood alongside the periscope. Poised at the ladder which led to the submarine's bridge were two lookouts, dressed in black. With Tolliver were Tom Friday, Wes Clayton, and Jake Stock. Stock also was dressed completely in black. He wore a forty-five automatic in a holster at his waist, and slung over his shoulder was a black leather case which contained a flashlight, note pad and pencils, and a supply of emergency food rations.

The word came up from the control room. "Standing by to surface, Captain."

"Very well. All ahead two-thirds!"

The sailor on the submarine's annunciator responded as he rang up the new speed.

"Answering all ahead two-thirds, sir."

"Very well."

Tolliver's hand moved to the alarm which signaled diving and surfacing for the submarine, and, as he pressed the button three times, his voice snapped the command.

"Surface! Surface! Surface!"

Ooga! Ooga! Ooga!

Below, the men on station in the control room were instantly galvanized into action. The boat's diving planes were hydraulically shifted to a hard rise position, forcing the bow of the submarine upward, and ballast tanks were blown clear by high-pressure air, giving the submerged vessel a buoyancy which drove it toward the surface.

"Passing five oh feet, Captain!"

"Very well."

Jake Stock felt himself touched with an only vaguely defined sense of awe which he invariably experienced upon returning from beneath the sea. It was an emotion he did not pretend to understand, although he recognized it as having some sort of religious significance for him, and he glanced at the faces of the other men in the conning tower, wondering if they shared that feeling with him . . .

"Passing four oh feet, Captain . . . Three five feet . . . three oh feet . . ."

Now the *Mudskipper*'s bridge was clear of the water. Tolliver snapped, "Crack the hatch!"

One of the sailors was up the ladder leading to the bridge, and he reached up and undogged the hatch handwheel with a swift, practiced motion. Air spewed in through the slightly open hatch, and, with it, sea water. Jake Stock drew a deep breath, welcoming the sweet clean smell of the outer world.

"Pressure one-half inch." This came from the control room.

Then, "Two five feet, Captain. Holding steady."

"Open the hatch!"

As the sailor finished undogging the hatch and snapped open the safety latch, Tolliver was already on the ladder behind him. The heavy bronze hatch cover heaved open with a loud rush of air as the latch was released, swinging upward to be secured in a vertical attitude. Seconds later, Tolliver was on the dripping bridge.

With deliberate slowness he scanned the horizon for a full three hundred and sixty degrees. He could just barely make out the dark line of the Hokkaido coast off the submarine's starboard quarter. There was nothing else to be seen. The search completed, he leaned over the bridge intercom.

"Lookouts to the bridge. Executive Officer and Mr. Stock to the bridge."

A few moments later, Jake Stock stood beside Tolliver. Wes Clayton had taken over the con of the submarine and was ordering the opening of the main induction valve and the beginning of a low-pressure turbo blow. The *Mudskipper*, her tanks still partially filled with water, wallowed sluggishly in the moderate sea. Stock heard the loud thumping sound as the main induction valve, through which air for the diesels was taken into the boat, opened. Seconds later, another sound came from below— like the screeching of some mortally wounded jungle beast. The turbo blow was under way, forcing air into the ballast tanks to give the submarine a more seaworthy attitude.

It was a good night for what had to be done, Jake Stock thought. There was a moon, but it was mostly obscured by a heavy cloud cover. The night air was chilly but not uncomfortable. His eyes, made ready for the darkness by the red night-vision goggles he had worn for the last half hour before reporting to the conning tower, searched out the shore line which lay in a low, almost flat line against the horizon to the starboard of the *Mudskipper*. It looked very far away.

Tolliver was back on the intercom. "Bridge to conning tower. Give me a radar sweep all around, then get me a range to land." He turned and called up to the two lookouts on their perches alongside the periscope shears. "Stay alive up there. Sharp eye out for aircraft."

A moment later the report came up, "Radar shows all clear, Captain. Range to land is four miles."

Tolliver turned to the Executive Officer. "All right, Wes, you say we can get in to a mile from shore without too much trouble?"

"Yes, sir. The charts aren't the best, but if we go in slowly and keep the fathometer going, we ought to be okay."

Tolliver bent over the intercom speaker again. "Come right to three five five. All ahead one third. Tom, keep a close eye on the fathometer. If it gets as low as four oh feet, stop and back emergency. And keep that radar on constant search."

"Aye, aye, Captain."

Tolliver straightened and stared in silence at the long slender forward section of the submarine as it knifed through the black water, cutting a gleaming phosphorescent path. His face, barely illuminated by the faint reddish glow from the conning tower below, was a mask, the sharply defined features set in hard, unvarying lines, his eyes intent on the distant shore. After several minutes he spoke.

"Wes, you keep the con now. We ought to be in position to launch the boat in about twenty minutes. Get the boat on deck and inflated, and see that those radar reports keep coming. Just because we haven't run into any night search planes up here so far doesn't mean there aren't any."

"Shall we start putting in a battery charge, Captain?" Clayton asked.

"Might as well."

Tolliver took Jake Stock by the arm and led him aft to the cigarette deck at the rear of the superstructure.

"All right, Jake," he said, "let's go over it one more time."

Stock took a deep breath and nodded. He felt tight and edgy. More than anything in the world just then he wanted a cigarette, and the knowledge that he would not have one until this was over and he was back aboard the *Mudskipper* did nothing to improve his disposition.

"It'll probably take us between half an hour and forty-five minutes to get ashore, depending on how strong the tide is running. By the time we get the boat concealed and reach the tracks—say another half hour. There's no way of knowing exactly how far from the shore the tracks are, so that's a guess. I'll want to spend about an hour scouting the area around where we're going to plant the bomb . . ."

"And be sure to mark the place so you can find it again," Tolliver said.

"Yes, sir. And mark it."

Tolliver nodded. "Then to get back to the rubber boat and back to the sub should take another hour, give or take a little. Right?"

Jake Stock's teeth showed in a fleeting grin. "If everything goes okay, and we don't have any trouble finding you."

Tolliver tapped him lightly on the arm. "Don't worry, Jake. We'll be here. Beginning at three hours from the time you shove off, we'll run a series of signals with the flashlight up here on the bridge, every five minutes—three shorts and a long."

"And if anything goes wrong ashore—"

"Nothing will go wrong, Jake, but, even allowing for the off chance that something should happen to delay you, we'll be here until daylight and right back here on the same station tomorrow night as soon as it is dark."

Stock nodded. "It'll be okay, Captain, but, if anything happens out here—if for any reason you have to get out of here—or dive—or whatever—if we don't find you, we'll head back to the beach and hole up and wait until tomorrow night."

"There's nothing around here, Jake, but this submarine and that train—I can feel that in my bones—and after tomorrow night there'll be only us."

"Captain!" It was Wes Clayton. "The SD radar has a contact!"

Tolliver and Stock stared at each other. The SD was the submarine's air search radar. Tolliver moved forward quickly, brushed past the Executive Officer, and bent over the intercom.

"This is the Captain. What's the range and bearing of that SD contact?"

"Fifteen miles, Captain. Bearing three two zero now. Seems to be closing slightly."

"Very well. Keep an eye on it and keep the reports coming."

He straightened and moved back along the port side of the bridge, his eyes straining into the darkness. Jake Stock came up to stand beside him, and Tolliver laughed nervously.

"Wouldn't you know they would pick tonight to show up? Probably some sort of military transport plane. If they flew regular antisubmarine patrols here, we'd have seen some sign of them before this."

"No change in plans, Captain?" Stock already knew the answer to the question, and he wondered why he had bothered to ask it.

"Of course not, Jake. For one plane that doesn't have a chance in the world of spotting us? Forget the plane."

They could hear the crackle of the intercom, and a moment later, Wes Clayton called back to them. "SD reports range ten miles now, Captain. Bearing is pulling ahead, but not much. It could be closing our track."

Tolliver acknowledged the report brusquely. Then he called, "How long before we reach our launch position, Wes?"

"Maybe ten minutes, Captain."

"Come on, Jake." Stock followed Tolliver forward where they looked down on the forward deck where several men were busy with the rubber boat. An air line had been run up from the low-pressure manifold in the control room and used to inflate the cumbersome-looking craft. Tolliver leaned over the bridge cowling and shouted to the men.

"How's it going down there?"

One of the men, a Chief Boatswain named Al Jacobs, called back cheerfully, "Just about ready to ride in, Captain. We're checking it for leaks now."

"Not exactly a luxury liner, Jake."

"It'll do, Captain." He was growing impatient with Tolliver's presence and his insistence on talking to him about the mission.

"You know something, Jake. I've been on the boats almost since the beginning of the war, and I'll have to admit something to you. This is the first time I've actually seen one of those rubber boats. I knew we were supposed to have one aboard, but this is the first time there's ever been any occasion to use one."

"Another first, Captain?"

"Yes." Tolliver shot a quick glance at him. Stock's face was stolid, and Tolliver chose to ignore the edge he had recognized in the question.

"Yes, another first. Is Baldwin down there on deck?"

"Yes, sir. He's helping check out the boat." Stock had selected Freddie Baldwin to accompany him on the scouting mission. He had confidence in the hot-tempered boy from Baltimore, despite the fact that this was Baldwin's first patrol on the *Mudskipper*. He was strong as a young ox, and that strength would come in handy rowing the boat through the mile or more of coastal waters.

"SD contact range is six miles. Bearing three four five."

Tolliver grunted, uninterested. "He'll cross our track and never have any idea we're here."

Jake Stock stared into the stygian blackness off the *Mudskipper's* port bow. The presence of the Japanese airplane out there did nothing to improve his mood.

And then Tolliver was at him again. "Remember, Jake, try to get as many details as possible. Like the gauge of the tracks, the surrounding countryside, the general terrain—anything. So we'll have as complete a picture as possible. I would like it better, Jake, if I were going ashore, because I want to know what it's like. I'm counting on you to be my eyes for me."

"Yes, sir." Stock was sick of it. I am part of a damned game, he thought. This has nothing to do with the war. It has only to do with keeping this man happy, of giving him something to do, something he can write about in that report of his. I am dressed up for a part in a kid's make-believe game, and I'm a grown man with a wife and a kid of my own back home.

His self-enforced rule against thinking of his wife dissolved without warning, and the full sweet memory of her flooded him. He surrendered himself to that memory, yielding to every aching sensation of his recollection of her. His eyes closed, and his big hands gripped the bridge cowling in desperation.

She is the one thing, he thought, the one thing that makes any sense in a crazy world . . .

Then, slowly, straining to the effort, he forced the floodgates of memory shut and drained her from his thoughts. Fleetingly he had included his son, but there could be no real image of him. Jake Stock had never seen the infant boy who now bore his name.

And he was calm again—and empty of emotion—and ready for what lay ahead.

"I'd better get down there, Captain. Anything else before I shove off?"

"No." Tolliver chuckled softly and slapped his hands together. "You're on your own now, Jake."

Stock started down the ladder which led to the submarine's main deck, and Tolliver called after him, "Enjoy your liberty, Jake."

"I'll try, Captain."

"And, Jake . . ."

"Yes, sir?"

"Take care, Jake."

In that instant, Stock could almost believe he detected some trace of doubt in Tolliver's voice, almost . . .

"I will, Captain."

Then he dropped to the deck, and, as he moved forward to join the men working on the rubber boat, he could hear the report coming up to the bridge over the intercom.

"Contact ten miles, Captain. Dead ahead and moving away."

Five minutes later, Jake Stock and Freddie Baldwin were alongside the *Mudskipper* in the rubber boat. The submarine lay gently wallowing in the black waters slightly over a mile off the coast of southern Hokkaido. There was a brief exchange of goodbyes. Stock looked up at the submarine's bridge and saw the dimly silhouetted figure there raise one hand in salute. Then he grasped his wooden paddle firmly and muttered to his companion.

"Let's go, Freddie."

He pushed the boat away from the rounded hull of the submarine, and the two men dipped their paddles into the choppy water.

On the *Mudskipper*'s bridge, Jonathan Tolliver checked the luminous dial of his watch. It was twenty-one thirty-five.

Four

⚓

THE SINGLE HEADLIGHT of the locomotive cut through the darkness for a distance of only a hundred feet or so ahead of the train. And the fog which was moving in would soon cut down that visibility. From his seat in the locomotive's cab, Inouye stared morosely ahead at that little patch of track and at the enveloping blackness beyond and all around it. The night run back to Nemuro from Kushiro was not a pleasant one. Inouye possessed a sense of the important, a concept of the relative value of things and of places, and, inevitably, it was more significant to go from a lesser to a greater place than to do the reverse. Nemuro was a place of little importance. Kushiro was a great city by comparison.

In Nemuro, Inouye lived alone, keeping to himself. There was no person in Nemuro with whom he could converse or share any part of himself. Being a man destined and intended for the sea, he badly needed the company of worldly men—men whose commerce was with far-flung and exotic ports of call—men who possessed a sense of national purpose and a grasp of international complexities. In Kushiro, there were such men. Yet when he had talked with men in Kushiro that morning, they had spoken of the progress of the war with flat, dead voices, mouthing the same boasts of inevitable victory with which the war had begun, but lacking in conviction now.

Listening to them, Inouye had felt shame and anger—helpless emotions, both of them. He was ashamed of his own lack of active participation in the war, although in his better moments, he could convince himself that the train was important and that he was needed where he was. His anger, blind and unreasoning and untutored, was directed against the hated enemy—the Americans.

Only once in his life, when he was a boy, had Inouye seen an American. He remembered the man only vaguely—tall, impossibly tall, and with very white skin. He had come to Inouye's village which was north of Nemuro, and the children had followed him about with avid curiosity. Once, the tall American had stopped and talked to the children in his strange, harsh language, and he had smiled and held out his hands with sweets in them. The other children had taken them, but Inouye alone had held back, and the American had come to him and urged the sweets upon the boy. And Inouye had finally yielded to the temptation and snatched at them and run away. When he was away from the sight of his playmates he had tasted the sweets and found them to be more delicious than anything he had ever tasted. But in his delight with the candy, he had realized that it was wrong—that the tall, pale stranger was not his friend and that to accept gifts from him could bring only evil. And then Inouye had thrown the rest of the candy away and, all alone, had wept at the loss.

From that moment he had hated Americans, and he had gloried in the magnificent victories of the Emperor's forces over the Yankee dogs. In his private world of dreams, he had envisioned himself going one day as a conqueror to the land of the tall Americans and being followed about by their white-faced children and tossing them handfuls of sweets—not in love and kindness, but in scorn and hatred.

Now, despite the continued boasts of the men in Kushiro, Inouye knew that the war was going badly. It was even conceivable that the Americans might gain an ultimate victory over the forces of the Emperor. There were rumors of great naval battles and of losses of many ships. In the port of Kushiro he had noted that there were fewer and fewer merchant ships. He had seen sailors from those ships, and their faces bespoke fear and defeat.

And Inouye, with his own love of the sea, with his own private dreams of the decks of a mighty vessel heaving beneath his feet, with his growing sense of an unrequited need for an active participation in the war—Inouye began to live in his own recurring fantasy of glorious battle and death in the service of his Emperor, as his ancient train moved through the black night and neared the stretch of track which ran alongside the coast.

"Can you see anything, Lieutenant?"

"Not a thing, Freddie. Keep paddling, but take it easy. We should be there just about now."

The fog had moved in swiftly, without warning, and for the past twenty minutes the two men had been propelling the rubber boat blindly, unable to see for more than an arm's length in any direction.

"I hope to God we didn't get ourselves turned around in this soup," Freddie Baldwin muttered.

That possibility had occurred to Jake Stock, but he said nothing. It was not the only unpleasant thought that had occurred to him since he and Baldwin had pushed off from the side of the *Mudskipper*, but he had kept them to himself and would continue to do so.

"What's eating me, Mr. Stock, is what we do if this damned stuff don't clear a little before we're supposed to head back to the boat. We won't stand a Chinaman's chance of finding them like this."

"We'll find them, Freddie. Don't worry about it."

Suddenly his paddle scraped against something solid. "I think we're in, Freddie!"

He dipped the paddle into the water again and felt it digging into what felt like sand.

"Yeah!" Baldwin whispered. "I feel it too!"

Minutes later they were dragging the rubber boat across a narrow beach of what felt to be more like ash than sand. The beach ended abruptly in a tall rough grass about twenty yards from the water's edge.

"We could hide the boat in this grass, Mr. Stock."

"Yeah. It's as good a place as any, I guess."

"How're we gonna find it again in this damned fog?"

Stock choked off the sharp reply which came automatically to his lips. The trouble is, he thought grimly, Baldwin is asking me the same damned questions I'm asking myself, and I don't have any answers.

"We start gambling as of now, Freddie." He forced himself to sound casual. "Come on, let's get the boat in this grass."

When the boat was clear of the beach, Stock drew a deep breath and, cupping the beam with one hand, switched on his flashlight.

"Jeez, Mr. Stock, what if somebody sees that?"

"In this fog, Freddie, there's damned little chance any-one'll see it, and that's something we'll have to risk. We're going to have to use our lights a little, so don't sweat it." Kneeling on the beach beside the place where they had hidden the rubber boat, Stock scooped up a handful of the wet ashlike sand. "This ought to do it." He stood up. "Take over, Freddie, and build us a little sand castle to mark the place. I'll hold a light for you."

The sailor dropped to his knees and went to work. Stock shielded the light as best he could. Baldwin looked very strange—like a big kid playing at the beach, his thick, powerful hands scooping and patting the wet sand into a mound.

Watching him, Jake Stock could not escape the idea of his son in another time, another world, a world and time when a father might take his son to the beach and teach him to swim and watch him playing happily in the sand, not on a fog-shrouded hostile shore but in the bright light of a summer's day. And he silently vowed a promise to the son he had never seen. *I will give you all of the things. All of the things a father can give. All of the things I could never have.*

"How's that?" Baldwin had constructed a mound about two feet high.

"That'll do. I just want to be able to spot this place in a hurry in case we need to."

Baldwin traced an awkward *B* on the top of the mound and got to his feet with a grin. "Okay, what now?"

Stock switched off the light. "We'll move on inland until we reach the tracks first. Then we mark our location on the track so we'll be sure to be as near here as possible when we're ready to leave. Then, I'll work in one direction along the tracks for about a mile and you do the same in the opposite direction. We'll want to spot anything the least bit out of the ordinary along the tracks, so make a note of anything you see—any sign of life, any buildings, water tanks—anything out of the ordinary about the way the tracks are laid out."

There was a moment of silence, intensified by the blackness of the night and the thickness of the fog. Finally, Baldwin asked in a low voice, "What do we do if we run into any company?"

"That's not likely," Stock said, "but if you do, be sure you see them instead of the other way around. Remember, we're looking for things. Nobody around here is looking for us. That gun you're wearing isn't to be used except in an emergency, and I mean a real emergency." His own hand dropped involuntarily to the gun at his waist. It felt heavy and unnatural. How long had it been since he had fired a gun, he wondered. He and Baldwin were removed from their proper environment. A sailor had no business playing commando. "What I mean is, don't go off half-cocked and start shooting at shadows. We're here to get the layout and get our butts back to the boat as quickly and as quietly as possible. So take it easy."

"Mr. Stock . . ."

Baldwin's face was barely discernible. Stock muttered, "Yeah, what is it?"

"That beef me and Kenestrick had the other day—the one you busted up . . ."

"Later, Baldwin. We don't have time to gossip."

He regretted his words instantly. Freddie Baldwin had come to the point of talking to him as another human being—perhaps because Stock had selected him for this mission—perhaps because in the loneliness of the fog-shrouded night on a strange and hostile shore, a man would reach out for a friend, no matter who he was with. As long as they were concentrating on the business at hand, Stock could relax and be himself, but Baldwin had tried to raise a matter which had to do with their relationship as officer and enlisted man, and Stock automatically shied away from it.

"Let's go," he snapped, wanting to say it in a different way but unable to be anything other than a manufactured officer, a mechanical authority who must control by the book because he had been created by the book.

"Yes, *sir*." And Freddie Baldwin, who had been very close to being his friend, reverted to being his underling.

Silently the two men moved away from the spot where the rubber boat was hidden. They walked through the high, rough grass for twenty or thirty yards. The footing was not good, and, twice, Baldwin stumbled and fell, cursing softly each time. Then they were clear of the grass and moving over what was mostly rocky soil and going uphill. Finally they reached what seemed to be level ground. The fog was still as heavy as before, and Stock was keenly aware of the oppressive silence of the night which seemed to close in on them from every direction. They were in another world, cut off from reality, a world on whose barren surface it seemed unlikely that any other humans had ever walked before.

"I'm going to use the light," Stock said, "just for a minute, to see if we can spot anything. Those tracks shouldn't be far now."

"Wait!" Baldwin's hand clutched suddenly at his arm.

"What is it?"

"I thought I heard something."

Stock strained to listen, but there was nothing.

"You're imagining."

"No! I can hear it!"

"What?"

"Sounds like a plane maybe."

Again Stock listened intently, and this time he too caught the faint, almost indiscernible sound. It seemed to come from above all right, but he knew the ears could play strange tricks in the darkness.

"It's getting louder!"

It was a plane. Stock tried to locate the direction from which it came, and he was disturbed to find that his own sense of orientation was confused. They had come from *that* direction, and the sound seemed to be coming from there also. That would mean the plane was over the water. Could it be the same one they had picked up before they left the *Mudskipper*? And if so, why was it back? It seemed to be angling in toward land from out where the *Mudskipper* awaited their return. If it was a radar-equipped night search plane, it might have detected the submarine, and there was little doubt that the submarine's radar had picked up the plane.

Now the plane's engine sound was louder.

"What d'you think, Mr. Stock?" Baldwin had automatically dropped to his knees as though to hide himself from the plane.

Then, with a sudden roar, the plane was passing almost directly over them, flying low, and Stock crouched also. He could almost imagine he actually saw the plane, but there was still only the fog and the blackness. It passed over them, moving inland, the roar of its engine fading away into silence.

"What if he spotted the sub?" Baldwin whispered.

Stock shrugged away his own feeling of concern which that same question, asked silently of himself, had brought. "Then maybe we've got problems, Baldwin, but we'll worry about that when the time comes. Let's go."

He switched on his flashlight and let its beam play ahead of them as they moved inland once more. They had gone only a few yards when he saw the tracks.

"There they are!"

With the discovery of the tracks one problem was solved for Jake Stock. He realized that, without knowing it, he had been hoping that they would not locate the tracks, that the other-world quality he had felt on this bleak and unknown shore would prevent him from finding them, that the train did not really exist, that he could return to Tolliver and tell him that the train, like his plan, was a fantasy and that the *Mudskipper* could go back to doing the job it was intended to do. But the tracks existed. They were real, and he knew the train was real, and that he was to be the instrument of destruction just as Tolliver had planned.

"Okay, Freddie, let's go."

He made a heavy mark on one of the crossties with a piece of chalk he had brought for that purpose. This would be the point to which he and Baldwin would return.

"Now keep close to the tracks," he warned. "Don't go wandering off so you can't find your way back here. If you spot anything, make a note of it—what it is and as near as possible how far it is from here. Check your watch."

Baldwin turned his own light on the dial of his watch. "Okay."

"Set it at twenty-two sixteen. Check?"

"Check."

"Okay. We'll meet back at this spot in exactly one hour. Twenty-three sixteen. That should put us back to the boat in plenty of time."

"If the damned boat's still there."

"It'll be there. Now shove off, Freddie."

For a moment the two men stood facing each other in the darkness. Stock could sense the mute appeal of Baldwin for some word of comradeship, but the moment passed and no words were spoken. Silently each man, the victim of his own fears and doubts and unanswered questions, turned his back on the other and moved slowly away until the night had swallowed him.

In the *Mudskipper's* conning tower, Jonathan Tolliver sat hunched over the plotting table, the mug of coffee which Roy Watson had brought him half an hour earlier still untouched. A few feet away, Wes Clayton watched him uneasily. The old man was obviously in no mood for conversation. Ever since the low-flying Japanese plane had forced them to dive, Tolliver had been sitting there, silent and grim, his face a mask of bottled-up fury in the weird red light of the conning tower. For a while, Clayton had thought that Tolliver was going to ignore the plane and remain on the surface, but when it became obvious that the Jap was picking them up, he had reluctantly given the order to submerge.

"Time?" It was the first word Tolliver had spoken in fully ten minutes.

Wes Clayton hurriedly held up his watch to the light. "Twenty-two forty-five, Captain."

"That gives us a little less than two hours before they're due back."

"Yes, sir."

Tolliver raised his head and looked up at the overhead. He seemed to be straining to see beyond the maze of pipes and conduits, through to the world above the surface of the sea which was some eighty feet above him. Clayton had seen men look upward in that way, usually men who were new to the boats and whose eyes in unguarded moments revealed their raw and naked yearning for the clean, fresh air of the world from which they had been excluded. But there was no fear in Tolliver's eyes—only an urgency, an energy which strained toward a task which needed completion. It was as though he could sweep aside the things which stood between him and the completion of that task by the sheer force of his will.

"We'll wait another ten minutes, Wes. Then we'll go back up."

Clayton stirred uncertainly. Questioning a decision of Jonathan Tolliver was not to be considered seriously, even under the best of circumstances, but Clayton had the instinctive desire of a submariner for the protection afforded him by the depths of the sea. He could see no reason for exposing the *Mudskipper* to that Jap plane any more than was absolutely necessary.

Still he knew enough to phrase his objections with caution. "Do you figure that plane is gone for good, Captain? I mean, if he did pick us up, and I don't see how he could have missed us, won't he probably be still searching this area?"

If Tolliver heard him, he gave no sign. "I'll want the two best lookouts on the boat up there with me, Wes. And I want you to stay on the radar in here. We can finish putting in the charge between now and the time Jake and Baldwin get back."

Clayton sighed. "Aye, aye, Captain. Ten minutes."

Tolliver got to his feet and slapped his hands together sharply. "On second thought, Wes, let's do it now. I'm tired of waiting." Without further concern for the Executive Officer, he moved toward the ladder which led to the bridge. "Stand by to surface! All ahead two-thirds!"

The fog had lifted a bit, but visibility was still less than fifty yards. Tolliver leaned forward, his hands resting lightly on the bridge cowling. Behind him, up in their perches alongside the periscope shears, the two lookouts were intent on making continuous sweeps from dead ahead of the submarine, through a full one hundred and eighty degrees to dead astern. It was virtually impossible for either of them to see anything in the fog, and each man knew this, but neither of them questioned their orders or considered doing anything but carrying them out to the letter—not when those orders came from Jonathan Tolliver.

The *Mudskipper* was maneuvering in a tight circular path whose center was the point of rendezvous to which Jake Stock and Freddie Baldwin were to return. It was not necessary for Tolliver to give commands to his helmsman. Indeed, there was no need for any words, for any sound other than the soft, muffled noise of the machinery which came from the vitals of the submarine.

But there were words in the mind of Jonathan Tolliver, words for the night which surrounded him:

Tis now the very witching time of night,
When churchyards yawn and hell itself breathes out
Contagion . . .

And his lips moved to form the words, though he made no sound, and he savored the feel of the unspoken poetry

74

on his lips. He saw himself as Hamlet, as the Renaissance man living out his terrible act of vengeance against—what? The answer was somewhere out there in the fog, just beyond his grasp. But it was really not important. His vengeance did not really need a motivation. It was complete within itself, a self-contained entity which belonged to him and to him alone.

Contagion!

There is a force in words, he thought, just as there is a force in me. Just as there is a force in a bullet, a bomb, a torpedo. In a war, my force is married to their force, but when the war is over, the Navy will have nothing left for me. Perhaps then, I will go to some quiet school—a boys' school in New England—and I will teach poetry, teach boys the force of words.

It was an odd thought, and he enjoyed it for its very incongruity. Why not, he thought. He liked being with young boys. He would like sharing with them his own love of words as he might have with a son of his own. He had no son. He would never have a son.

His hands tightened on the cowling, and, for a moment, he felt a sickening wave of fatigue rising within him. To drive it away, he forced himself to look at the luminous dial of his watch.

It was twenty-three fifteen.

Jake Stock had been walking for nearly forty minutes, moving slowly and cautiously along the railroad tracks, using his light every few minutes to make a quick search around him. There was nothing to be seen but rocks and clumps of brush on either side of the tracks. He knew that it was time to retrace his steps to meet Freddie Baldwin, but there was something hypnotic about the tracks and the fog and the darkness of the night. Something kept drawing him on. There was no sense of distance. He had the distinct feeling that at any moment he would reach something, touch something—something which had life in it, something of substance which could bring back reality to his world . . .

At first he was only vaguely aware of the vibration on the tracks. Then there was a sound—faint, but unmistakable—and then he saw the headlight. He knew it was the train, still far away, and he stood in the center of the tracks and watched as the vibration grew stronger, the sound louder, the light, shining through the fog, brighter.

He stood and watched it come until, with a quick and angry movement, he leaped away from the tracks and ran to conceal himself behind a large clump of brush about ten yards off the tracks.

Then the train was there, rumbling by his hiding place. He could see the locomotive fairly well, although the fog gave it a ghostly appearance. He could see the man in the cab of the locomotive, leaning forward, eyes fixed on the tracks ahead. When Jake Stock had been small, he loved to go down to the railroad tracks which passed near his home and wait for the trains so he could wave at the engineer and the fireman. He would take a box of animal crackers and a piece of cheese—rat cheese his mother called it—with him, and he would sit in solitary splendor on the little sloping hillside and await the train. And the fireman would always return his wave, and sometimes the engineer, when he was not too busy, would wave also— and Jake Stock would be transformed, for the moment, into a man in a man's world of iron and steam.

The train was gone. It was not a large one—only a few cars, and they looked ready for the scrap heap. That locomotive, though, seemed to be in good condition. It was the first foreign train Stock had ever seen, and he found the experience disturbing. Trains, somehow, were very American—like ice cream and hot dogs and baseball. He wondered what the Japanese word for train was . . .

He switched on his light and checked his watch. It was twenty-three twenty. He was already four minutes late for his rendezvous with Baldwin. He hoped Baldwin had seen and heard the train in time to get to cover. Quickly he took out the notebook and made a record of the time the train had passed him. Tolliver would want that for sure. Then he returned to the tracks and started walking as rapidly as he could back to where he was supposed to meet Baldwin. He did not use his light again.

And in the fog-shrouded night, as Jake Stock walked along the tracks, not fifty yards from him the old man, Kurita, and his patrol settled themselves after having watched the passing of the train. Their only excitement of the night was over. They did not see the American who walked those tracks in the trail of the train. They only huddled together and cursed the darkness and waited for the coming of another day.

Five

⚓

AFTERWARDS, when it was morning, the boy Takeo was convinced he had actually felt the train as it roared through the night. This was what had awakened him. He could believe this because it meant he and the train had a kind of bond between them—they were in communication—an understanding existed between them. Therefore, it was not surprising that he was able to *feel* the passing of the train, even while he was asleep, and that the train could, in this way, awaken him.

It was true that, as he lay on his straw mattress earlier in the evening and waited for sleep to take him, his thoughts had been of the train and only the train.

The train returned during the night!

The train, with fire belching forth from its belly like a dragon, racing through the night!

The train! The night!

He was awake instantly, his eyes opened wide, all of his senses alert. There was no sound in the house except the gentle snoring of his mother and the fierce, gasping, old man's snoring of his grandfather. And the darkness seemed to have dimension—thickness and weight which pressed in on him. Takeo knew little of darkness. In his house everyone went to sleep soon after night came, and Takeo almost never woke until it began to grow light.

Although in recent years no one had had the time to tell him stories, out of his very early childhood there remained the memory of tales about the night—of demons who walked about in the night—and of *other things*, too horrible to be described, which lived in the night world.

The room was completely black. It was as though there was no room, no walls to define space, only infinite and endless blackness. Takeo thought that were he to get up from his mattress and begin to walk, in any direction, he would undoubtedly walk on forever into a void which would simply swallow him up and make him a part of the night.

Why had he awakened? There was *something*. He sat up on his mattress and tried to remember in which direction the door was. It must be this way—if he got up very quietly and walked very softly and kept his hands carefully stretched out in front of him so that he would not stumble or fall or make a noise which might awaken his mother and grandfather—if he walked thus . . .

His hand reached the door!

Very carefully, very slowly, he pushed the door open and stepped outside into the night. A heavy fog lay over the land, and Takeo knew that, on such a night as this, the demons and *other things* must surely be all around.

But why had he awakened?

Shivering a little, partly from the chill of the night air, but mostly from the dread of the night things, he stood, his head held high, his eyes and ears straining against the darkness and the silence. And his eyes could see nothing, but then his ears heard the sound of the whistle, echoing faintly through the night, and Takeo knew the train was returning even at that moment, that were he in his place by the tracks he would be able to see the train and hold up his hand in greeting to the man in the train, and perhaps the man would see him also. And perhaps . . .

But that was stretching the dream too far. He put that possibility from his mind. Still he stood there in front of his house and listened in case the whistle should sound again, but there was nothing more. The train had passed by for that night, and now only the darkness and the silence and the fear remained.

Finally Takeo slipped quietly back into the house, closed the door, and made his way back to his mattress. Once his grandfather stirred, interrupting the savage rhythm of his snoring to mutter unintelligible words in a shrill, complaining voice which trailed away into snorts and groans and eventually back into the familiar snoring.

Takeo lay on his back, his eyes opened wide, and thought about the train. He was beginning to suspect that the train had awakened him, that, if he willed it to do so, the train could awaken him any night as it passed. This pleased him, and he was convinced that he would sleep no more that night, because there were too many wonderful thoughts to be enjoyed there in the darkness where he could be anything he wanted, do anything, go anywhere . . .

And then he fell asleep.

But sleep merely expanded the freedom of his thoughts, exalting them into dreams, and in his dreams he did what the waking Takeo would not even allow himself to think of doing. He did wave at the train, and the man in the train did see him and wave back at him, but there was more, much more. Because the train stopped, and the man who ran the train held out his hand to Takeo, and Takeo went to him and took his hand, and he was drawn up into the interior of the great locomotive which was made of gold and silver and shone like the sun. And the man who ran the train sat upon a throne which was covered with jewels, and he took Takeo up upon that throne with him and allowed Takeo to touch with his own hands the gleaming *things* which made the train go, and Takeo and the man and the train roared away into the night, leaving the farm behind and forgotten.

And there was no fear of demons or of *other things* which walked in the night. Because the train was mightier than any of those things, and Takeo had become a part of the train, and nothing could hurt him.

The figure loomed up in the fog. Jake Stock's hand dropped to his gun.

"Is that you, Mr. Stock?"

Stock switched on his flashlight and directed the beam at the figure. Freddie Baldwin was crouched, one hand leveling the 45 automatic at Stock.

"Who did you think it was?" He switched off the light. "For Pete's sake, put that gun away before it goes off and hurts somebody."

"I couldn't see very well. I figured it was you, but I didn't want to take no chances."

"What would you have done if it wasn't me?"

Baldwin laughed nervously. "Jeez, I don't know. Probably dropped my teeth. I've been waiting here about ten minutes, but it seems like ten hours."

There was no reproach in that statement, only a genuine relief, and Stock was grateful for this. He had been reprimanding himself ever since the train had passed for being late starting back. If he had been the one who had been kept waiting, he knew very well he would have chewed Baldwin out.

But he had been the one who had violated his own explicit timetable. This underscored another in the long list of deficiencies Jake Stock knew himself to possess as an officer. He knew how to kick a man in the rear but he was still afraid to kick himself in the presence of an enlisted man. To make a mistake was not a frailty Stock had learned to live with as an officer, and mixed with his gratitude for Baldwin's not calling attention to the fact he had been late for their rendezvous was an instinctive distrust of the enlisted man's charity.

His reaction was to read reproach into Baldwin's words and to react accordingly

"If I was late, you ought to know there was a damned good reason, so knock off the bellyaching!"

Baldwin stared at him. "I'm not—"

"I said knock it off! Now let's get out of here."

"Yes, *sir*."

As they moved away from the tracks in the direction of the sea, neither man broke the hostile silence which this exchange had created. Stock walked in the lead, using his light from time to time as they picked their way through the high rough grass. Somewhat to his surprise they located the rubber boat without difficulty. When it was in the water, they paused for a moment, still silent, and stared out into the black and empty expanse of fog-shrouded water. Somewhere out there, Stock was thinking, is light and warmth and life, but standing here it seems impossible.

Stock had always had great difficulty accepting the reality of things he could not actually see. There were times, when he lay beside his wife in their bed, when he would suddenly be seized with panic for fear she did not actually exist. Even touching her could not totally reassure him, and he would switch on a light so that his eyes might see her, and she would awaken and protest sleepily —but gently, because of all the people in Jake Stock's world, she alone understood his fears and his great need for reassurance.

Then, to his surprise, he learned that Freddie Baldwin recognized that fear also—or did he simply share it?

"I guess they're really out there, Mr. Stock, but it sure as hell looks empty, don't it?"

Stock nodded, aware that Baldwin's words had checked a rising feeling of panic in him, and for the second time he had reason to be grateful to the other man.

"It's okay, Freddie. They'll be there." He hesitated, struggling to get past his own barrier. "I keep telling myself . . ." He had succeeded, a little, and that made him feel better. He was able to laugh and sense Baldwin's response. "Come on, let's get this baby under way. As far as I'm concerned this is a lousy liberty port."

When they were clear of the rocks and paddling slowly out into the darkness, talk came easier.

"You know what I felt like when I was walking down those tracks, Mr. Stock, in this damned fog? It was like driving a car back home when it's snowing, and the snow keeps coming at you and after a while you get sorta hypnotized. If that damned train hadn't come along and snapped me out of it, I think I might still be walking along those tracks."

"Did you find anything out of the ordinary?" Stock asked.

"Nothing much. I guess I must've gone about a mile or so, and about half way along the fog lifted a little in this one spot, so I took off inland a little just to check it out a little. It's mostly farm land from what I could tell and lousy farm land at that."

Stock grinned. "I didn't know you were a farmer, Freddie. I thought you grew up in Baltimore with all those white doorsteps."

"I did, but a couple of summers while I was playing ball in high school, the coach lined up jobs for some of us on farms down on the eastern shore. I got to know a little about farming."

"Any sign of people?"

"I think maybe I saw a couple of buildings of some kind off in the distance, but I couldn't tell whether they were houses or barns or what. Then the fog closed in again, and I figured it was best not to go stumbling around any closer to them."

"You say that was about half a mile from where we started?"

"Yes, sir."

They paddled on in silence. The fog seemed heavier over the water than it had on land. Stock checked the time. It was already twenty minutes past midnight. Tolliver and the *Mudskipper* should already be on station and sending out periodic signals for them, but it would take the rubber boat at least another half hour to reach the vicinity of the submarine, assuming they were not being carried off course by the current, which seemed to be running much stronger than when they had come ashore.

Sitting there, paddling that ridiculous rubber boat, and

remembering the plane, Jake Stock suddenly flared with a helpless anger at the whole crazy business. He and Baldwin were playing a game, a game created by Jonathan Tolliver for his own amusement. Assuming that they did get back aboard the *Mudskipper* safely, why not give a report which would force Tolliver to call the whole thing off? They could report heavy security forces stationed in the area—something—anything . . .

He glanced over his shoulder at Baldwin. What did Baldwin think of the idea of blowing up the train? How would he react if Stock suggested making a false report on conditions ashore?

"That train coming along caught me by surprise, Freddie. Did you see it in time to get out of the way?"

"Yes, sir. Got behind some rocks and watched it go by."

"Not much of a train, was it?"

"No, sir. You think that's the one the skipper means to get?"

"I doubt there's any other train on that line."

"Jeez, Mr. Stock, it really felt creepy, you know—watching it go by, I mean. I could see the engineer when it passed me."

"So could I." Baldwin sounded shaky. If there was ever to be a time, this was it.

"Mr. Stock?"

"Yeah?"

"How big a bomb d'you figure it'll take?"

"I don't know for sure, Freddie, but—"

"Man oh man!" Baldwin chuckled. "Won't that be a kick? That Jap won't know what the hell hit him, and when that boiler goes up it'll be like the Fourth of July! *Wham!*"

Stock's paddle bit viciously into the black water.

"Yeah, Freddie. It'll be like the Fourth of July."

"Mr. Stock . . ."

"What is it?"

"Listen . . ."

Both men stopped paddling. Stock strained to listen. Then he could hear it—the same faint sound of a plane they had heard before. It was up there again . . .

"Okay, Freddie. Stay loose and start keeping a sharp eye out for the light."

"They won't show no light with that Jap up there!"

"They'll show a light, Freddie. We may all get blown out of the water, but the Captain'll get us back aboard. Now come on!"

They started paddling again, and their eyes strained into the darkness to catch some sign of the submarine, and, overhead, the sound of the plane's engine grew steadily louder.

"Range is now five miles, Captain, and closing!"

Jonathan Tolliver clamped his jaw tightly shut and nodded without a verbal acknowledgment of the radar report.

Wes Clayton's insistent voice repeated, "Five miles and closing, Captain!"

"I heard you!" Tolliver turned to the quartermaster, French Turnage, who stood beside him on the bridge with the shotgun signal light. "Send that signal again."

Turnage rested the barrel of the light on the bridge cowling and pressed the trigger—three long and three short flashes of light.

"Range three miles! Still closing!"

Instinctively the quartermaster stopped sending the signal and turned toward Tolliver, only to be met with a harsh, "Who told you to stop? Keep sending!"

Turnage's eyes rolled unhappily, but he had been with Tolliver long enough to know how the game was played. "Aye, aye, sir."

"Looks like he's really homing in on us, Captain!" On the intercom, Clayton's voice was touched with panic.

If Tolliver heard, he gave no sign. Without stopping his own probing search of the darkness, he called up to the lookouts, "See anything up there? Now stay alive!"

"Not a thing, Captain."

"Two miles and closing fast!"

Tolliver's hands squeezed the binoculars as fear pounded at his temples. He could feel the tight hard knot in his belly growing larger, and he gloried in the sheer joy of his own secret terror. This was just what he had been needing, he knew. This was the food he thrived on.

"Keep sending that signal!"

"If that Jap plane sees it . . ." Turnage was desperate. What the hell was the old man doing flashing a damned light with a Jap coming in on them!

"You heard me, Turnage. Keep sending!"

"One mile!"

The men on the bridge could hear the plane now. It was coming in from the port quarter, flying low . . .

"Lights, Captain!"

He whirled to the lookouts. "Where?"

"About three points off the starboard bow, Captain. There they go again!"

Tolliver's glasses located the faint signal. Three long and three short!

"Right five degrees rudder! Recovery team on deck on the double! Come on, Turnage, keep sending them that signal. I want to be sure they see us."

"Aircraft, Captain!" The port lookout screamed the warning. "Dead astern!"

"Lookouts below!"

The two men were already dropping from their perches and scrambling past Tolliver.

"Give me that light, Turnage, and get below!" He took the light from the quartermaster. Now he was alone on the bridge. He forced himself to focus his whole attention on the tiny flashing light which was now almost dead ahead of the *Mudskipper,* sending its signal over and over again. The roar of the plane's engine filled his ears as it passed over the submarine, and he braced himself for the explosion he knew would follow—but there was nothing. The miracle had happened! The pilot had waited to be sure of his prey before dropping any bombs. He would be back, but he had given Tolliver a margin, and it might be enough . . .

Down below him on deck, the men responsible for getting Stock and Baldwin and the boat back on the submarine were waiting.

"Stand by to dive in a hurry as soon as they're on board," Tolliver snapped into the intercom speaker.

"The plane is turning, Captain. Heading back!"

Now he could make out the rubber boat—and the men in it.

"All stopped! All back one-third!"

The submarine's forward movement slowed, ceased altogether as the backward thrust of the screws ground it to a halt.

"All stopped!"

This was the critical time. Dead in the water, the *Mudskipper* presented the Japanese pilot with an ideal target. If his radar was any good at all . . .

88

And he was coming in!

Tolliver could see Jake Stock and Baldwin being hauled bodily up onto the deck and hustled toward the gun access hatch.

"The boat!" The fools were forgetting the rubber boat. His head was on fire, and he was screaming, "Get that boat!"

Then the sound of his own voice was drowned in the consuming roar of the plane's engine.

WHAM!

The submarine heeled over violently. The deck was going from beneath his feet, and Tolliver felt himself falling, knew unreasoning terror, felt sharp, blinding pain—then nothing . . .

"Are you okay, Captain?"

Wes Clayton's worried voice came at him from a great distance. He tried to move his lips—to form the words . . .

"Captain? Take it easy, Captain."

Then he could see Clayton, bending over close to him—and, behind Clayton, slightly out of focus, he could make out Jake Stock.

"We pulled you off the bridge, Captain. The Jap dropped one more bomb, but we were under by then. There's no serious damage . . ."

There was something he must know. "The boat . . ." Now he was able to speak! "Did you get the rubber boat? We'll need it . . ."

Clayton glanced quickly over his shoulder at Jake Stock, then nodded. "We got it, Captain . . ."

Stock's voice was thick and difficult to understand. It was like the fog, Tolliver thought.

"Freddie Baldwin got the boat for you, Captain . . ."

"Baldwin?" he heard himself saying.

"He got the boat for you."

A great feeling of relief swept over Tolliver. It was all right, then. There was no serious damage, and the mission could be carried out as planned. The train would be destroyed. He had been right to take the risk.

"Baldwin," he repeated. "Baldwin got the boat?"

"Yes, Captain," Stock was saying. "Freddie Baldwin got the boat for you."

Tolliver smiled. "Good for Baldwin," he said finally. "I'll put him in for a citation—maybe the Silver Star. You too, Jake. Just get that train . . ."

Then, inexplicably, Jake Stock was laughing. Tolliver could see his face distorted—hear the great roaring, gasping laughter. Then it was gone. Jake Stock was gone. There was only an awful silence. He struggled to make things come clear.

"What—what's the matter with him?" he asked. "What's the matter with Jake?"

Wes Clayton spoke very gently. "Baldwin got the boat back, Captain, but he didn't make it himself. When that bomb hit—he didn't make it back. Somebody saw him go over the side, and we were already on the way down. Baldwin is dead, Captain . . ."

Six

⚓

INOUYE REQUIRED little sleep. He would generally reach his solitary dwelling in Nemuro shortly after midnight, prepare himself a simple meal, and then retire for no more than five hours of sleep before arising for the morning trip back to Kushiro. He had disciplined his body to get along with no more sleep than this, although on occasion he would enjoy an hour's sleep in Kushiro.

He prided himself on this ability to do with a minimum of rest. It was, for Inouye, a further mark of his true nature, which was that of a warrior, trained to carry on his duties without pampering his body. He did not often dream when he slept. Inouye's dreams were mostly confined to his waking hours, because then he could be master of those dreams. Dreams which came while he was asleep he found frightening—mysterious fantasies which lurked in the dark and forbidden recesses of his mind which were beyond his power to control.

On this morning, however, a dream came to Inouye as

he slept—a dream he had never had before. In the dream he stood on the deck of a mighty ship. All around him were men like giants whose strange faces were as white as chalk. They appeared not to see Inouye, moving in some manner of solemn ritual all around him, but never looking at him. They gathered around something on the deck, and Inouye pushed his way through them to see what it was. There on the glistening deck of the great ship was the still form of what looked to be a man, wrapped completely in black. The men like giants seemed to be mourning for this man, their voices raised in a lamenting cry he could not understand. At last, Inouye could stand the mystery no longer, and he knelt beside the form to uncover the face.

None of the giants made any move to stop him. Their wailing continued as though Inouye did not exist. Then he pulled away the black wrapping and looked at the face of the man.

It was Inouye's own face!

And he wanted to scream. His mouth opened wide, and his lips moved, but no sound came forth. To his horror, the mouth of the man with his face opened also, and the dead lips moved, but still there was no sound as silent horror echoed silent horror.

Then the giants, still mouthing their mournful cries, moved past—moved through Inouye as though he were not there and took up the still form of the thing which possessed the face of Inouye and carried it to the side of the great ship and let it fall into the black void which was the sea. And Inouye, rushing to the side of the ship, saw the form sinking into the black water, but the face—which was his own—still floated upon the surface of the water, the mouth still open and the lips still moving, struggling to bring forth sound . . .

"Aayeh!"

The scream finally tore from his throat and awakened him.

Wes Clayton cleared his throat and glanced down nervously at the text of the Committal service. He stood by the ladder in the control room of the *Mudskipper*. Beside him was Jake Stock. The regular control room duty section was in the compartment, while the rest of the officers and crew of the submarine who were not on duty had crowded into the crew's mess just aft of the control room. Wes Clayton spoke into the intercom.

"Unto Almighty God we commend the soul of our brother, Frederick Baldwin . . ."

The burial service is properly Tolliver's job, Jake Stock thought angrily. It was Tolliver who had sent him and Baldwin off on a fool's errand. The responsibility for killing Baldwin was his, and so was the responsibility for burying him. But Tolliver was still in his quarters, recovering from the blow on the head he had suffered when the Jap bomb went off.

"And we commit his body to the deep . . ."

Freddie Baldwin's body already belonged to the deep. Why not leave well enough alone? Desperately Stock tried to recall some detail of the dead man's face—his voice—something of him. They had been shipmates, and, more than that, they had ventured together on a strange and hostile shore. There had been something shared between them—fear and loneliness—but now nothing remained. It was as though the man named Freddie Baldwin had never existed.

"In sure and certain hope of the resurrection unto eternal life . . ."

Those words might just as easily be for Jake Stock. When he had heard Tolliver screaming at them to get the rubber boat below, he had started back, but Baldwin had been ahead of him. It was that thin a line between what was and what might have been. At this very moment Baldwin might be standing here listening to the words of the Committal being read for Jake Stock. And thousands of miles away, Helen would be without a husband—his son without a father—a second generation son born never to know his own father—and for what? Did Freddie Baldwin have a wife? A son?

"Through our Lord Jesus Christ. Amen."

"Amen."

The echoing word came from Jonathan Tolliver, who stood in the door which connected the control room with the forward passageway. His face was pale, and he held to the bulkhead for support, but his voice was firm and steady.

Wes Clayton closed the book hurriedly and started toward Tolliver. "You okay, Captain? I thought you needed the rest, so I went ahead with the service . . ."

"You did well, Wes. Thank you. Now I want to speak to the crew."

The men in the compartment fell back as Tolliver approached the intercom.

"Attention all hands . . ." Jake Stock marveled at the man's absolute control. "This is the Captain. First, let me assure you that I am not seriously injured. The Executive Officer has filled in for me in the sad task of committing the body of our shipmate to burial, but I am, as of this moment, assuming fully the duties of Commanding Officer of this submarine. Baldwin was my shipmate, as he was yours. He died serving in the highest traditions of the

Navy. I will recommend that he be awarded the Silver Star posthumously." He paused, and then continued, his voice noticeably stronger. "Until this past night, the *Mudskipper* has seen no action during this patrol. Many of you have grown restless and dissatisfied. Now, at long last, we have seen and faced the enemy. He has struck us a grievous blow, but it will not go unavenged. The mission in which Baldwin was engaged will be carried out, and the enemy will pay for his life with many lives. I give you my pledge to that!"

Tolliver turned and gripped Jake Stock's arm. "Get some rest, Jake. You're going to be busy tomorrow."

"No change in plans, Captain?" He fought to keep his voice steady.

Tolliver's eyes searched him quickly. "Change? Of course not, Jake. Come on now. I want to hear your report, but you'll need some sleep first. I'll have you called in about four hours." His voice dropped to a hoarse whisper. "No change, Jake! Understand that. *No change!*"

Seven

⚓

KOJIMA FIRST learned of the submarine when he reported to the officer on duty at the railroad station in Nemuro. Ordinarily the officer tended to be sullen and uncommunicative, but on this morning he greeted Kojima with a broad smile and an air of high excitement.

"There was a great battle," the officer said. "Very near here—in the early hours of the morning. One of our brave pilots surprised an American submarine very near our coast and attacked the cursed vessel. I understand the Americans tried desperately to escape, but our pilot was relentless and succeeded in dropping several bombs on the submarine, destroying it totally."

"Where did such a thing happen?" Kojima asked.

"South of here—off the coast quite near a place along which your miserable train runs." The officer laughed. "Perhaps it was taking place at the very moment the train was returning from Kushiro. I am not certain of the time, but the outcome is certain. It is a very great honor for all of the Emperor's forces in this area. It marks the first time the enemy has been engaged here, and to gain such a victory gives honor to all of us—even to such a miserable person as you."

The officer knew that Kojima had never been in battle. He himself had served briefly with the forces which had invaded the Philippines and won that early and glorious victory, utterly crushing the American armies. A leg wound had brought him back to duty on the home front, and with the passing of time the officer had managed to forget the fact that the wound he had suffered had actually been the result of an accidental firing of his own weapon and that, in truth, he had seen hardly any action against the enemy. He was destined, he knew, to serve out the duration of the war as an officer charged with the operation of the miserable supply station in this wretched little town. It was his duty to see that the catches of the fishermen were loaded aboard the train and that proper forms and reports were filled out periodically. Most of his time was spent in morose contemplation of the glorious military career he would never have. And in this process, he was given to taking his brief active service and enlarging it in his own mind into a gallant and colorful chapter. The soldier Kojima made an ideal audience for him. Kojima was a stupid peasant, a man whose life was mired down in the mediocrity of this post.

"What a glorious victory!" he exulted. "I tell you, soldier, I myself know how that pilot must feel this morning. I know what it is to come face to face with the enemy and destroy him. When I was in the Philippines—in that first great engagement—oh, if you could have seen that sort of battle, you would understand! We came ashore in great waves of men. The Americans fled before us, but soon, like rats they were compelled to try and make a stand against us. And they fought with the ferocity of trapped rats. I remember well the day I got this . . ." He slapped one hand sharply against his right leg. "My colonel had commanded me to take a small group of men and attack an American machine gun position. They were well situated and strongly defended, and we were outnumbered by at least four men to one."

This was the story his mind had invented and embellished and nourished until he had come to believe it to be the truth. "I led my men in a direct charge against the machine gun. There was no time for subtlety or strategy. The colonel had ordered the immediate destruction of that position. Most of my men were killed or wounded, but the charge went on. I myself came face to face with the Americans, and it was then I received this wound, but my strength that day was so great that I did not even realize I had been hit. I continued to charge, and I saw the faces of the enemy grow pale with fear. I saw them break and run, and I continued after them until they were either killed or utterly routed. It was only then that I saw I was bleeding. A bullet had struck me just above the knee, and I could barely walk, but still I gathered the remnants of my command and made it back to give my report to my colonel. When I had told him of our victory, I lost consciousness, and when I awakened, I was on the hospital ship. I learned later that my colonel himself had been killed that day. Otherwise, I know that I would have been decorated for that day's work.

"But I need no recognition, because I have that memory. I have the picture in my mind of the face of the enemy—filled with fear and the certain knowledge of defeat. That is my reward. And so, you see, I can understand how our brave pilot must feel this day. This is a thing which is shared by the brotherhood of brave warriors— the thrill of victory. I am truly sorry for you, soldier, for it is unlikely that you will ever know that thrill."

Kojima felt very small, very inferior—and yet, he knew with a great sense of shame, that he was glad to be where he was. He had never fired a gun in anger. He had never taken a life. He knew himself to be a gentle man, and he knew that somehow this was a disgrace. Sometimes he would have dreams about coming face to face with one of the enemy, and he would awaken in cold terror. Now he tried to share the excitement of the officer, to make himself a part of what had happened, but it was no use. All he could do was to nod dumbly, to make sounds of approval and humility. He could not project an image of himself as a participant in any act of violence.

The officer seemed to sense this, and he sneered at Kojima. "What a poor soldier you are! Why do I waste my time in talking with you?"

Kojima was grateful when the train's engineer made his appearance at that moment, and the officer limped off to tell Inouye of what had happened. Kojima quickly finished checking the morning's loading and climbed aboard the train, glad that his family had not come down to see him off that morning, then ashamed of being glad because the reason they had not come was that his daughter had been ill throughout the night—nothing serious, but still he must not find any joy in something which resulted from her illness. Seated inside the train, he could see the officer gesticulating excitedly as he told Inouye about the American submarine.

When the train began to move, Kojima settled himself for the trip, his gun held in his lap, his eyes staring out at the passing countryside, and his simple mind trying in vain to comprehend the nature of battle.

For the two men, Jonathan Tolliver and Jake Stock, the death of Freddie Baldwin had resulted in two quite different sets of conclusions. Stock had never been happy with Tolliver's plan to send a landing party ashore to blow up the train. He had been unable to completely identify his own reasons for this, apart from his belief that it was an unnecessary operation, one which involved more risks than the expected results could justify. Now, Freddie Baldwin was dead. Yesterday he had been alive. It was as simple as that. Like most submariners, Jake Stock had no experience with the isolated loss of a shipmate. On a submarine, it was tacitly understood that if one survived, all survived—if one died, then all died.

Now this axiom had been violated, and Jake Stock placed the responsibility directly at the feet of Jonathan Tolliver and his crazy idea about the train. What had begun as a dreadful complexity had been simplified. The mission of a submarine was to harass and destroy enemy shipping. Tolliver, for reasons of his own, had chosen to extend this mission, and the *Mudskipper* was neither equipped nor prepared to carry out the task Tolliver had selected. For this reason, Freddie Baldwin was dead. It could just as easily have been Jake Stock. And if they continued, then Stock and others would be risking their lives in a cause which was simply not worth it.

Jake Stock understood and believed this. He also understood and, in his way, believed in the set of rules which dictated absolute and unquestioning obedience to the orders of a Commanding Officer. He was, therefore, up early that morning and at work on the preparation of a package of explosives with which he would attempt to destroy the train for Tolliver. But his mood, as he worked, was not a pleasant one.

On the other hand, Tolliver himself had been rejuvenated by the events of the previous night—even by the death of Freddie Baldwin. Indeed, and to his own knowledge, he had been particularly bolstered by the death of Baldwin. Death, he admitted to himself, is the essence of battle. It is the reason for battle. Without death there can be no justification, no sense of purpose, no *purification*. It was not that he would consciously have wished Baldwin dead. He did not really know Baldwin, other than as a face—and a name. But Baldwin, by the act of dying, had provided Tolliver with a firm and tangible motivation for destroying the train. What before had been merely an act of destruction now became an act of vengeance, and this pleased Tolliver. Warfare, he thought, in its ideal form is always an act of vengeance. That was why this war, from the American point of view, was an ideal war. It came at a time when there was a need for war, and the Japanese had supplied a perfect motivation. There need be no pangs of conscience about this war. All that would ever be needed would be the magic phrase, *Remember Pearl Harbor!* And, Tolliver thought, we are free to destroy the enemy in whatever ways and wherever we wish. Only the most monumental and blatant act of national savagery could be marked against us in this war.

And the train, he thought—I have had bad dreams about the train. I know that there come times—afterwards—when I am haunted by things. But now I have a name, a phrase, *Remember Freddie Baldwin!* An eye for an eye, a tooth for a tooth, a train for the life of Freddie Baldwin!

The effect of Baldwin's death on the *Mudskipper's* crew had been nothing short of miraculous. Already that morning at least ten men had come to Wes Clayton, asking to be included in the landing party which would go in to blow up the train. Tolliver had made a brief tour of the boat, and in every compartment he had been able to feel the excitement and the eagerness for action.

Purpose! Motive!

Tolliver was at his desk, preparing to write a letter to Baldwin's mother. He had never written this kind of letter, and he might never again be called on to do so. It was rare, very rare, for a submariner to be killed—unless, of course, he was lost with all hands. This letter, then, should be composed with care . . .

He had gone through Baldwin's service record. It told him little of the dead sailor. He was from Baltimore, had a high school education, had played football, was interested in cars and had done well during his training period at New London, except for one minor escapade in a local bar. His religion was given as Lutheran.

Tolliver considered the blank piece of paper on the desk in front of him for a moment, then took his pen and started to write.

Dear Mrs. Baldwin:

Before this reaches you, you will have been notified of the loss of your son, Freddie. As his Commanding Officer, I want to attempt to convey to you and to all of Freddie's family and friends the feelings of myself and his shipmates at his death.

I knew your son well. He was a fine young man—capable, diligent, well liked by everyone aboard. He would often talk of his life before the war—of his high school football days, of his many friends in Baltimore, and particularly of you, Mrs. Baldwin. He was in every way a son of whom you can be proud.

He gave his life while performing a vital mission —one which even as I write this is being carried to completion because of his brave sacrifice. Someday I hope you will be able to know the full extent of his heroic action. I hope it will be of some small comfort that I am recommending him for the Silver Star as recognition of his bravery.

I know all too well that these poor words cannot lessen your grief. I do hope that in a small way they may help you to understand that your son gave his life in a highly important action and that he died performing his duties in the highest tradition of the service of which he was so proud.

We knew Freddie as a deeply religious boy, and, as I think of him, the old familiar and comforting words come back to me:

Oh, death, where is thy sting!

Oh, grave, where is thy victory!

He paused, leaned back, and considered what he had written. It had the right flavor, he decided—a bit florid in style, but this would be a letter Baldwin's mother would keep and treasure all her life. It would not seem florid to her, because she would want to believe every word that was written. It would do . . .

Carefully he concluded the letter and signed his name in a bold, slashing script across the bottom of the page.

It was interesting, he thought, as he folded the letter and placed it in an envelope. By the act of writing that letter, he had actually come to know Freddie Baldwin.

What had before been a cipher had turned into a man—a man, it was true, created by Tolliver for himself, but nevertheless a satisfactory image to recall—and to avenge . . .

Meanwhile, Jake Stock had recruited Amos Kenestrick to work on the construction of the bomb. His first act that morning had been to seek out the Chief Torpedoman. It had not been easy to approach him. The break between the two men caused by Stock's commission had been intensified by Stock's action after breaking up the fight between Kenestrick and Baldwin a few days earlier. He found Kenestrick in the after torpedo room.

"Amos, I want to talk with you."

Kenestrick glanced up from the magazine he was reading. "Yes, *sir*, Mr. Stock, *sir*."

"Knock it off, Amos."

"Knock what off, sir?"

Stock fought down his anger. "Okay, Amos, I know how you feel about me, and perhaps I don't blame you. That's not the point now. I need you to work with me on putting this bomb together."

Interest flickered in Kenestrick's eyes. "You're really going to blow that damned train?"

"It looks that way."

Kenestrick laughed softly. "The old man is really a catbird, you know that? Who else would've thought of a submarine going after a train?"

"Not many people, I guess."

"You're damned right. Not one in a thousand." He stopped and looked at Stock suspiciously. "So you figure you need me on this?"

"You know more about explosives than anyone on the boat, Amos."

"Yeah, that's right. More than anyone—including you, sir."

Stock held his voice steady. "Exactly. So, let's get at it. I figured you could work back here."

Kenestrick shrugged. "As good a place as any." He hesitated. "Look, Lieutenant . . ."

"Yes?"

"Well, it's this way, Lieutenant, seeing as how you and I are going to have to work pretty close together on this thing for a while—I mean, if I help build this thing, then I'm taking it for granted that I get to go along for the fun. That's right, isn't it?"

Stock nodded. "If you want to go, Amos . . ."

"I want to go! You're damned right I want to go!"

"Okay, then you go."

"Good! Then, here's what I wanted to say, just so's there won't be any misunderstanding. I'll build you a bomb, and I'll go along to watch the fireworks—because Baldwin was a shipmate of mine—because the old man is the greatest skipper in this navy, but not because of you, Lieutenant."

"Okay, Amos, if that's the way you feel . . ."

"That's the way I feel! And could I say just one more thing, Lieutenant—seeing as how we were once fellow peasants—one thing off the record?"

Stock's throat was tight and dry. "Go ahead."

"Okay, let me make it clear that I hate your guts, Lieutenant. If you want me working with you under those conditions, then let's get started."

It was a challenge to which Jake Stock would ordinarily have responded violently. As a fellow petty officer, he would have broken Kenestrick in half. As a commissioned officer, he should have put him on report for rank insubordination. As something in between, he did nothing.

"Let's get to work, Chief," he said.

Kenestrick grinned with open contempt. "Yes, *sir.*"

The lines were thus clearly drawn between the two men, and from that point on, each understood his position. Stock knew Kenestrick well enough to be certain the Chief Torpedoman would do a good job, despite his enmity. He would have preferred it some other way, but this would have to do.

"I figured," Stock said, "that we'd pull some torpex out of one of the fish and use that for the charge."

"Good enough. We're not about to shoot those fish at anything on this damned run."

"What about the detonator?"

"Same thing," Kenestrick said. "We'll just borrow one from a torpedo."

"Good. I'll leave the actual explosive packaging to you then."

"Yeah, you do that. How did you figure to set it off? You going to use a timed fuse?"

"No, I thought about using a microswitch and connecting it to the actual bomb. We can place the switch right on the track, with the bomb just beside the track. It ought to be as small as possible and covered in some dark stuff to reduce the chance the engineer will spot it. The headlight on that train isn't too powerful, and it throws a pretty narrow beam."

"You actually saw the train then, when you and Baldwin were ashore last night?"

"Yeah, I saw it."

For the moment Kenestrick seemed to forget his animosity. "What'd it look like?"

"Like a train, Amos. What else?"

"I mean—was it like our trains back home? How big was it?"

"Not big." Stock did not want to remember the train. He wanted the train to be an unreal thing—but he could see it, in spite of himself. "Smaller than our trains, I think. There couldn't have been more than half a dozen cars on it, and they looked pretty well beat up—as much as I could tell. It was foggy . . ."

"Boy oh boy, when that thing goes off, those Japs won't know what the hell hit them! Probably they'll think it was some plane that dropped a bomb on them." Kenestrick laughed. "That's par for the course, you know. We go in and knock off a train, and the fly boys'll probably get all the credit for it."

"The locomotive, though," Stock continued, unable to stop now, "the locomotive looked good. Somebody had really been taking care of it. I could tell that, even in the fog. It was all painted and shining. And I could see the engineer. I had a feeling about him when I saw him— about him and his train . . ."

Kenestrick glanced at him with a wolfish grin. "What the hell's eating you, Lieutenant? You sound like you don't think much of the idea of blowing up that train."

Stock looked up, startled. Then his face hardened. "Do I, Chief? Come on, let's get to work. The Captain is going to be wanting his bomb."

And in the conning tower of the *Mudskipper*, Jonathan Tolliver was at the periscope, watching the progress of the train as it made its morning run from Nemuro to Kushiro. It was right on schedule, and, as he watched it, Tolliver could feel a familiar excitement growing within him.

Eight

⚓

TAKEO SHIVERED when he thought how close he had come to missing the train that morning. He had almost overslept, and when he had realized this he dashed out of the house without eating his breakfast, running all the way to the tracks and arriving there only a moment before the train passed. The man who ran the train did not even glance his way, and this made Takeo very unhappy. It was a cloudy, gray, and discouraging morning, and Takeo watched the train as it vanished in the direction of Kushiro. The day stretched ahead of him, long and miserable, with nothing to look forward to, unless—unless that night . . .

He did not want to return to his house. His mother would be waiting there to scold him for running out before he had eaten, and his grandfather would join in with his querulous old man's scolding. Neither his mother nor his grandfather understood him. Takeo believed with all his heart that his father would have understood him, had he lived. It was his hope and belief that the man who ran the train would also understand him, if he could only know him.

To delay his return home, he walked along the tracks, following after the train, stretching his legs to step from one crosstie to the next, and then hopping up on the rail and balancing himself as he walked along it. He could almost feel the train on the soles of his bare feet, feel the life which the passing of the train had transmitted to the steel. Could it be his imagination? He knelt beside the rail and placed his ear upon it. It was true! He could actually feel and hear the pulsating life of the train!

Then he saw the chalk mark.

It was in the form of a large cross, marked on the wooden crosstie in white chalk. Why Takeo should have noticed it he could not tell, but he found it very interesting. Hesitantly he reached out one finger and touched the mark, and it smeared a little from his touch. Getting to his feet, he quickly examined several other nearby crossties, and none of them bore any chalk marks. Why had this particular one been marked? He had seen no workmen in the vicinity for several months. And yet, surely the mark had been made by someone—and recently, or else it would have been washed away by the rain. Only a few days ago there had been a heavy rain. He returned to the marked crosstie and studied it carefully. Except for the chalk mark, it was no different in any apparent way from any of the others.

Someone had selected that spot—and had made a mark there—someone, or *something* . . .

This prospect was more to Takeo's liking. He immediately discarded the idea of some person and concentrated on the possibilities involved with the concept of *some-*

thing. The demons and other things which walked in the night were not all evil. There were good demons, and the cross mark had the look of some sort of magic sign. Suppose—just suppose it had been put there for his eyes only. Why had he walked along the tracks this morning? Usually he went straight home once the train had passed. But on this morning he had walked, and on this morning he had stopped at this particular spot, and on this morning he had knelt down so that he could not avoid seeing the mark!

It was quite clear he had been meant to do all these things on this particular morning, but *why*?

Then he remembered the night before when he had awakened so mysteriously, just in time to hear the passing of the train. He remembered his thoughts about going out in the night to watch the train. He remembered his dream—the train stopping and taking him aboard . . .

And now here was a mark to which he had been led. The mark of the two lines crossing each other at a point. One line, he reasoned, could be taken to represent the line along which the train traveled each day. The other line could represent Takeo's life. And they crossed each other at this point! It was at this point that Takeo's life and the train would come together!

His heart pounded furiously. He wanted to run, to shout, to call after the train and to tell the man in the great locomotive that he understood. Perhaps that man himself was in reality part demon—a good demon—who had somehow managed to make the mark even as his train roared over this very spot. If only there were some way Takeo could answer . . .

Kneeling beside the chalk mark, he wet the tip of one finger, rubbed it in the earth and gathered a supply of mud on it. Then, with great care, he drew a circle around the cross. He had to repeat the process several times before the circle was distinct.

"I understand!" he whispered. "I know the meaning of your message, and I will come here. I will come tonight. I promise!"

Then he rose and began to gather small rocks which he piled into a heap a few feet away from the tracks. That would help him find this place, even in the dark of night.

Suddenly the sun broke through the gray clouds, and Takeo felt his face touched with its warmth. It was a further sign!

He stood looking down at the chalked cross with the circle around it, and once again he said—quite loudly this time and clearly and unafraid, "I will come tonight. I promise!"

"No, sir, I don't see any point in increasing the size of the landing party," Jake Stock said. "It seems to me the fewer guys we have, the easier things will go." He hesitated, then added, "Besides, there's no point in risking any more necks than we have to."

He and Tolliver were in the latter's stateroom. Stock had left Amos Kenestrick working on the construction of the demolition package when Tolliver had sent for him. Now the *Mudskipper*'s Commanding Officer regarded Stock with a frown of annoyance.

"No point risking any more necks, Jake? Meaning what?"

"It's just that—after what happened last night . . ."

"So now I am to blame for that?" Tolliver's voice rose slightly.

"I didn't say that, Captain."

For a moment Stock thought the other man might actually strike him. His eyes glared, and he seemed about to spring from his chair. Then he was himself again. Whatever it was had passed as suddenly as it had come. When he spoke again, his voice was calm and patient.

"In a war, Jake, men are killed. Baldwin died in the line of duty. It could happen to any one of us on any day at any time. True, it was a freak thing—once in a thousand times a plane comes in like that. It happened, and it's done with. Your job is to go in and blow up that train. My job is to see that you're given the men and the equipment to get the job done—no matter what other freakish things might happen. I think you should have no fewer than seven men, counting yourself. That cuts down the margin for error and accident. That Japanese pilot may have reported us destroyed. Very probably he did, because it was what he wanted to believe. But even if he did, there may very well be someone who will want to make sure. Before last night we had the advantage of absolute surprise. We may still have it, but there is a chance—a chance that what happened out here has alerted the enemy throughout this area."

"Perhaps," Stock ventured, "if we held off for a couple of days . . ."

Tolliver's eyes glinted. "No, Jake. That's what you're really after, isn't it—holding off a few days, then a few more days, and then forgetting the whole thing—is that it?"

"Captain, I . . ." He met Tolliver's stare for a moment and then nodded. "Yes, sir. I guess that's right."

"I see." Tolliver got to his feet, moved over to the curtains at the door and pulled them shut. When he turned to face Stock again, his face was tight with anger. "Court-martial! That's what I could do to you for what you've just said. Any other officer on this boat would jump at the chance I'm giving you, and this is the thanks I get—you turn coward on me, just when I—"

"Wait a minute, Captain!" Stock could feel his own temper building.

"Shut up! I said I could have you court-martialed for cowardice, and I could make it stick!"

"You know me better than that, Captain!"

Again the storm passed from Tolliver, and he laughed as he moved past Stock, slapping him lightly on the shoulder. "Relax, Jake. I'm needling you. Of course I know you better than that. I don't take a Chief Petty Officer and put him in for a commission because he's a coward. I was just pointing out to you what I could do.

"I picked you for this job because I knew you were the best man for it, and I'm sticking with you. Because, Jake, I know you'll do my job for me whether you like it or not." He leaned forward. "But I want you to like it, Jake. I want you to go in there tonight because you feel the same way I feel—that it's our duty to hit the enemy and to keep on hitting him in any way we can, wherever and however we can as long as he still keeps fighting us. I want you to feel about that train the same way you'd feel about a Japanese destroyer that was trying to blow us out of the water. You know that feeling, Jake. Remember when we hit those two destroyers in one day?"

"Yes, sir. I remember."

There was no point in trying to explain to Tolliver the difference. He did remember that day—his own savage joy when he had heard the torpedoes exploding against the sides of those destroyers. He had yelled and laughed and pounded the men around him. *But that was different!*

"Of course you remember, Jake. A Japanese destroyer —a Japanese train—it's all a part of why we are here."

But the destroyers were trying to kill us, Stock told himself. But if that was to be his argument, what about merchant ships, tankers, troop ships? He had exulted in the destruction of those also. Why was this train different? *Why?*

He looked at Jonathan Tolliver, realized that Tolliver was also staring at him, and yet, he knew that neither man was capable of really seeing the other. Each was seeing something of his own—something, Stock knew with a shock, which had the quality of madness in it. There is no answer, Stock knew in that instant. He wants the train destroyed for reasons I can never understand or accept—for reasons which have nothing to do with the fighting of the war. He pretends this is not true, but he is lying. The real reason is deep down within the man, and perhaps he does not know it himself. Just as my reasons for not wanting to destroy the train are deep inside of me. I know—I believe they are good reasons, but I cannot identify them. I cannot admit them, even to myself, and so I am a little mad as well as Tolliver. We are hopeless and ridiculous opponents, because neither of us is capable of exposing his true motivations. And so the thing will be done. The train will be destroyed, and more men will die—the Japanese engineer, most certainly, and others—perhaps some more of our men will die—perhaps I will die, because Tolliver's word is my law, and his unspoken reasons must prevail over mine . . .

"You see that, don't you, Jake?"

"Yes, sir. I see."

Tolliver smiled, and Stock recognized the pure relief in

that smile and was shocked by it. This was a man he no longer knew—a man who had once been like a god. Now he was a man who was wrong, but who would prevail—because for a little while he *had* been a god. It was as simple as that. Jake Stock could not stop him from this senseless act of destruction. No man could stop him. Only a miracle could stop him now . . .

"Captain from conning tower!"

The voice which crackled over the intercom startled both men. Tolliver stared at the speaker on the bulkhead for a moment, then reached up and pressed the key.

"This is the captain."

"Captain, we've just spotted smoke on the horizon, bearing three two five!"

For several seconds Tolliver did not speak. Then he replied, "I'm on my way up. Change course to head for the smoke."

He turned to meet Jake Stock's gaze again.

"Looks like business is picking up, Captain."

Tolliver nodded. "Perhaps." At the door to the stateroom, he hesitated. "Jake, get back there and check on the progress on that bomb. I want it ready in plenty of time."

"If we have to go to battle stations, Captain . . ."

For an instant, Tolliver's eyes clouded. "We'll cross that bridge when we come to it."

"Yes, sir."

"All right, Jake, let's hop to it." Tolliver's face was tight and drawn, and he seemed to want to say more. Instead he turned and headed for the control room. Jake Stock followed him, watched as the *Mudskipper's* Captain climbed the ladder to the conning tower, and then continued aft toward where Kenestrick was working on the bomb.

One thought pounded away at his mind. If there were a ship up there—if Tolliver had to go after a ship and attack it—then the train might be spared.

What had he thought—a miracle? Perhaps this was the miracle!

Nine

⚓

It was the day for the officer from Kushiro to come for
Kurita's report, and the old man was troubled. Last night
two things had happened. As he and his patrol had been
waiting for the long night to end, there had been two explosions. They seemed to come from the sea. The fog had
been too heavy to see anything, and Kurita was not really
certain he had heard anything, for he had been dozing at
the time. But some of the other men had said they heard
explosions, and so Kurita assumed he must have heard
them also. However, it was not the explosions which troubled Kurita most. If they had indeed come from the sea,
then they had nothing to do with him. He could not be
held responsible.

What troubled Kurita was much less tangible than the
actual and audible sounds of explosions. Some time earlier, while he had been sitting apart from his men, staring
into the night, fighting to remain awake—he had suddenly *felt* something. Kurita was a simple old man. He

had no words or even thoughts with which to identify complexities or subtleties. But, sitting there in the darkness, his mind struggling with the task of remaining awake, his body chilled by the night air, his stomach tight with hunger—Kurita had been suddenly and inexplicably wide awake and tense. It was as though a hand had gripped his shoulder, warning him of some presence. And yet there had been no one, no sound, nothing but the dimly discernible figures of his own men huddled a few feet from where he was sitting. He had grasped his rifle tightly and got to his feet, listening, wanting to go out to search for whatever it was, but he did not. He was afraid —not only of finding something in the night, but also of *not* finding anything. Indeed, the latter fear was the greater of the two.

And so Kurita remained where he was, the hair rising on the back of his neck—until the feeling had passed. And when the explosions sounded, he had forgotten the feeling, and the two events had in no way been associated in his thoughts until the next day.

Then, waiting to make his report to the officer who, he knew, despised Kurita and despised equally his own task of having to make the periodic and meaningless inspections of such areas while other soldiers were fighting gloriously on faraway battlefields—waiting for this, Kurita did put the two events together, and in his heart he knew them to be related. But how could he explain this to the officer? How could he say, "I *think* there was *something*." Or, "I *felt* there was *something*." How could he say such things without having to explain why he, as the leader of the patrol, had done nothing to investigate? He knew very well what the officer would do. In all probability he would take the rifle away from Kurita and put one of the other men in charge of the patrol. It was better to say nothing . . .

On this day, much to Kurita's surprise, the officer appeared to be in very good spirits. He actually smiled when the old man was brought before him to give his report.

"The patrol," Kurita said, "has made its regular inspections of the assigned area with great diligence each night during the past week, and all has been quiet and in order."

The officer laughed, an unprecedented thing for him. It was, Kurita thought, a very unpleasant laugh. "Do you mean you heard nothing out of the ordinary last night, old man?"

Kurita was now faced with a truly agonizing choice. The officer might be referring to the explosions. If he knew about them, and if Kurita had not heard them, then he would most certainly lose face and perhaps even his position as leader of the patrol. On the other hand, if he had heard them and had not reported them, then he would have proved negligent in his duty which was explicitly to report any and every happening which was in any way out of the ordinary. It had been stressed to him when he was given his position that it was not his place to make any evaluation of any event. Except in the case of an actual invasion by the enemy, he himself was to take no action but merely make a report of what had happened.

But the officer, miraculously, was in too high spirits to force Kurita to either of the two humiliating confessions.

"The enemy was out there last night, old man." He pointed in the direction of the sea. "One of our planes was flying on patrol, and he detected the presence of an American submarine. With great courage and daring, he swooped in to attack the devils, and with two bombs he utterly destroyed them, for they vanished beneath the water." He sighed happily. "What a glorious feeling that must have been for our brave pilot!"

Kurita was puzzled, and, seeing that he was probably not going to be punished for his negligence, he ventured a question. "But, sir, I do not understand. Last night a heavy fog lay over us here. How could a man in a flying plane see a ship upon the sea?"

Again the officer laughed. "How simple you are, you foolish old man! Have you never heard of the miracle of radar?"

"Radar?"

"Yes." The officer, who actually knew almost nothing of electronics himself, proceeded to explain the process to Kurita. "With radar, old man, one is able to see through fog and blackness—to see without eyes. Our magnificent plane possessed this radar, and with it the brave pilot could actually see the American devils on the sea below and attack them."

"Without seeing them with his eyes?" Kurita asked, amazed.

"Exactly." The officer was beginning to doubt his own explanation and so he hurried on, "He saw them—with the radar."

"Oh." Kurita considered this for a moment. "That is truly a miracle."

"It is with the aid of scientific miracles such as this that we will surely conquer the Americans," said the officer.

It seemed presumptuous to ask, but Kurita's curiosity got the better of him. "Do the Americans have this— radar—also?"

"Of course not!" The officer was indignant at the suggestion. "This is our miracle."

"To see without the eyes," Kurita murmured, fascinated with the idea.

The officer took his leave with a stern warning. "Old man, it is remarkable that you and your men did not hear the bombs which destroyed the American submarine. Remember this, it is your sacred duty to the Emperor to remain alert at every moment. If one American submarine was off our coast, there might be others. The very fact that such a submarine could come so near to our shores is evidence of the need for vigilance."

When the officer had gone, Kurita became fascinated with an idea. He could form only the vaguest picture of what the officer had called *radar*, but he did know that with this radar one could see without the eyes. This was, Kurita decided, very much akin to being able to *feel* the presence of something without actually seeing it. Last night, this had indeed happened to him. He had felt some presence, although his eyes had seen nothing. Was it possible, he wondered, was it possible that he, Kurita, actually possessed this miraculous power within himself? Could it be that he possessed *radar*? If so, then he had indeed *seen* something last night, though not with his eyes. There had been something out there in the night.

But what?

The trace of smoke on the horizon had grown into a ship, probably a freighter, hull down. Tolliver had been taking periodic observations for the past fifteen minutes. He had not yet called the *Mudskipper* to battle stations, a fact which puzzled the men with him in the conning tower.

It also puzzled Jake Stock, who had gone to the after

121

torpedo room fully expecting to hear the clanging of the general quarters alarm at any moment. But there had been nothing. Perhaps, Stock thought, the sighting had turned out to be a false alarm . . .

Amos Kenestrick had greeted the word that a ship had been sighted with a singular lack of interest. He was totally engrossed in the construction of the bomb—so much so that he seemed even to have forgotten his animosity toward Stock.

"Hell, Jake, I haven't had this much fun since I was a kid. I got me one of those chemistry sets one Christmas, and I damned near burned the house down, but did I ever have a good time!" He had already encased the explosive in an oilskin covering, and he patted it proudly. "This baby is gonna weigh more'n I figured—probably fifty pounds at least. I had to cut down an ammo storage cannister to hold the torpex, and I figured we'd better make it waterproof since we're taking it ashore in that rubber boat. But when this thing goes off, it'll tear that locomotive to pieces! I hope that Jap has a good head of steam in his boiler when she hits, because he'll go up like the Fourth of July!"

Stock nodded. "I wonder what the deal is on that ship."

Kenestrick chuckled. "I hope it's a false alarm. Hell, Jake, I've been in on plenty of ships getting sunk, but a train is something else again. Maybe the old man feels the same way."

In the conning tower, Jonathan Tolliver was rapidly approaching the time when he knew he must make a decision. The outline of the freighter was clearly visible now. Sound had picked it up and had the range at fifteen thousand yards. Tolliver had put Tom Friday on the Torpedo Data Computer just to get an estimated course and speed on the target, and the picture was reasonably clear. Provided the freighter maintained its present course and speed, the *Mudskipper* could get into attack position within the hour . .

"Up periscope!"

He grasped the training handles and snapped them down into position as the periscope slid up from its well. He could make out the masts of the freighter now. It was a small ship, probably not much over six or seven thousand tons. There was no telling what its cargo might be.

He shifted the periscope until the target was centered. "Bearing—mark!"

French Turnage, the quartermaster on duty, was reading the azimuth.

"Three five five."

"Right five degrees rudder!"

"Rudder is five right, sir."

He held the scope on the freighter. "Amidships!"

"Amidships, sir."

"Bearing—mark!"

"Dead ahead, Captain."

"What's our course?"

"Two five six, Captain."

"Steady on that."

The routine was automatic. He continued to track and close the target on reflexes, but his mind was busy with a consideration of the alternatives facing him. His duty to attack and sink the freighter was clear, but what would happen then? This attack, coupled with the plane's bombing them last night would alert the Japanese completely to his presence in these waters. There was no way of telling how much in the way of military forces they had left here, but if he attacked the freighter, they would be after him with everything they had. The pilot of the plane had undoubtedly bragged about destroying the submarine, but this would prove he was wrong. Getting the landing party ashore successfully depended on possessing an element of surprise.

Why the devil had a ship appeared today—after all this time of sighting nothing? It could be deliberate. The Japanese might be trying to draw him out by sending a worthless ship out to make sure the plane had done its job well the night before. They could be setting up the freighter as a decoy to trap him into exposing himself!

"Captain?" Behind him, Tom Friday spoke hesitantly.

"What is it?"

"You want me to call battle stations, Captain?"

He turned to stare at Friday. There was something going on, and he could not concentrate properly. For a moment, the idea that there was a plot against him flooded over him, and then—the possibility that Tom Friday was somehow a part of that plot . . .

No! That could not be!

"Captain . . ."

He shook his head to clear it.

"Just a minute, Tom. Up periscope!"

He bent over to peer through the eyepiece, but he already knew what he would see and what his reaction would be. Still, he had to be careful. He took his time, and he even managed to swear softly.

"Down periscope! Right full rudder!"

"What is it, Captain?"

He drew a deep breath. "It's a trap, Tom. I've been noticing how high that freighter was riding in the water. It was obvious she isn't loaded. So I had to find out why an unloaded freighter would be out here—where there hasn't

124

been a trace of shipping since we reached the area. I just found out . . ." He was completely confident of the lie he was to tell now. He did not approve of lying, but when there is a conspiracy against you, it is justified.

"It's a trap. I could see—just barely see—on the other side of that freighter—a ship. I couldn't tell for certain if it was a destroyer or a DE type, but I know why it's there. It's laying back, waiting to see if we are still around after last night. There're probably planes up there, too—a hunter-killer group. We'd fire our torpedoes at a worthless ship, probably not even in commission now, and then they'd have us nailed."

The sailor on the *Mudskipper*'s sound gear looked puzzled. "Captain, I'm not getting an echo from anything except the target."

Tolliver had the feeling of being closed in on all sides. He snapped angrily, "The destroyer—or whatever it is—is directly beyond the freighter. You wouldn't be able to pick it up."

"So what do we do now, Captain?" Tom Friday asked.

Tolliver watched the other officer carefully. "We lay low, Tom. We play dead. If that freighter isn't attacked, they'll believe that plane really got us last night. They know that if there's a submarine here, it couldn't miss spotting that ship. So they'll relax, and then tonight . . ."

Friday grinned broadly. "Tonight, then, we get the train?"

Tolliver smiled. The man sounded sincere. Tom was all right. "That's right." The lie had worked! He felt wonderful. It had worked so well that he was beginning to believe it. There was a logic in it. Perhaps there was a destroyer beyond that freighter. "Tonight we go in and get the train!"

"You think the Japs will be looking for us anyway, Captain? I mean, even if we don't take the bait?"

"It's a thought, Tom. Let's not take any chances. Take her down to one hundred and fifty feet and let's just lay low for a couple of hours." He turned to the sailor on the sound gear. He was still not certain about him. "Keep alive there on sound. You have the con now, Tom. I'm going below and see how Jake is coming along with the bomb."

"Yes, sir." Tom Friday had secured the Torpedo Data Computer. "Captain, do you reckon we ought to pass the word along? I mean, everybody on the boat is just raring to go since the word got passed that we'd spotted a ship up here."

"A good idea, Tom." Tolliver moved over to the intercom. "Now hear this. All compartments, this is the Captain. In the event that you are wondering what is going on, we have learned that the ship which was sighted a little while ago is a decoy. A Japanese destroyer was sighted, apparently just waiting for us to show ourselves in an attack on the target. We are not going to take the bait. Our procedure will be to lay low for the rest of the day and let the enemy think we were destroyed by the plane which attacked us—the plane which killed our shipmate, Freddie Baldwin. I want them to think the *Mudskipper* was destroyed, because tonight we're going after more exciting game. Tonight, for the first time in the history of submarine warfare, the crew of a submarine is going to destroy a train!"

He released the key and glanced at Tom Friday. "That ought to do it, don't you think?"

Friday grinned excitedly. "Captain, that *will* do it!"

The man on sound reported, "We just lost contact on

126

that target, Captain. I never did pick up anything else."

Tolliver's eyes narrowed. That man would have to be watched. "Very well. Stay alert, though. That destroyer is up there, and it might come looking for us on its own."

As he prepared to leave the conning tower, he found himself wondering what the cargo of the freighter had been. He did not regret the choice he had made. The train was more important. Now he knew beyond any shadow of a doubt that the train would have to be destroyed. To fail in that would mean he had deliberately permitted an enemy ship to escape without justification. He liked the pressure this placed upon him. Because to fail had now been rendered impossible—no matter what the cost.

This thought pleased him.

Ten

⚓

INOUYE RELAXED in the warmth of the bath, his eyes nearly closed, his body supported by the water. He sometimes came to the baths while he was in Kushiro and passed the time there while waiting for the hour when he must return with his train to Nemuro. There were also baths in that miserable village, but they could not compare with those in the city. This one was quite large and exquisitely appointed. From the windows of the room where food and drink were served after the bath, there was a magnificent view of the mighty peaks of O-Akan and Me-Akan, the twin mountains to the north of Kushiro. Inouye found solace and strength from coming to this place.

It was expensive, and ordinarily he limited his visits, but on this afternoon he had felt very strongly a need for the peculiar sense of comfort and well-being the place was able to give him. The dream he had had on the previous night disturbed him, and all through the morning trip from Nemuro to Kushiro he had been haunted by that dream.

Even the news he had heard upon reaching his destination of the destruction of an American submarine off the coast had failed to cheer him. Indeed, he found that news rather depressing. It was not that he was not pleased to hear of a victory, but the nearness of the action brought into sharp focus the fact that he, Inouye, was not actually a part of the war. It should have been Inouye who had destroyed the enemy. When the fighting was faraway, he could succeed in maintaining his fantasy of the warrior, but to have actual fighting and victory only a few miles beyond the miserable tracks on which he ran his train each day and night—to have the hated enemy engaged and destroyed perhaps at the very moment he was returning from Kushiro to the wretched village of Nemuro—this cut through fantasy and left Inouye only the dispiriting reality of his own ignoble position.

Now, half floating in the warm water, he gave himself over to a new fantasy—a fantasy born of his own dreams of glory, of the service to the Emperor toward which he yearned, of the news of death and destruction, of the subtlety and mystery of the languorous warmth of the bath—of the totality of his aspirations and frustrations.

And the truth which emerged for Inouye out of this new fantasy could not be denied.

I am going to die, he thought.

And when he had left the bath and been scrubbed dry and massaged by expert, powerful fingers—when he had donned the special kimono provided by the owners of the bath for such occasions—when he had sat and eaten the steaming food and drunk the saki—when he squatted on the grass mat and contemplated the mountain peaks in the distance, the thought remained with him.

I am going to die.

And the calm knowledge of this fact seemed to Inouye a beautiful thing

The landing party would consist of seven men, including Jake Stock. The rubber boat was designed to hold at least ten, but Stock knew that seven men and the equipment they would be carrying would come dangerously close to overloading the little craft. However, Tolliver had insisted, and he was past raising any objections to Tolliver's plans.

The men had been selected by Stock, and the wardroom had been turned over to him for a briefing of the landing party. It was shortly after noon when Stock, Tolliver, and Wes Clayton gathered in the wardroom with the six enlisted men.

Amos Kenestrick would be in charge of placing and securing the bomb itself. An Electrician's Mate, John Barringer, had rigged the microswitch which would detonate the bomb. It would be his job to place the switch on the track and make the final electrical connections to the bomb itself. Barringer was nineteen, a deceptively frail-looking boy. He had made two previous patrols on the *Mudskipper* and Stock considered him the best electrician on the boat.

Torpedoman First Class Milt Weslowski and Electrician striker Tommy Lyle would back up Kenestrick and Barringer. Both were husky men and would share the task of actually carrying the bomb from the boat to the tracks. The two other members of the party were Gunner's Mate Second Class Fritz Schroeder and Signalman Third Class Finley Tatum. They were rated the best night lookouts on the boat, and their job would be to stand guard over the rubber boat while the other five men took the bomb in to the tracks. Both Schroeder and Tatum would be armed with submachine guns. Stock would carry a carbine, and the other men would wear forty-five automatics.

Tolliver started off the briefing session. "I want to make one thing very clear at the outset," he said. "Each man here has been carefully picked as being the very best for this mission. Your selection was made by Lieutenant Stock and approved by me. In our opinion, you are the men we need to make this thing go. However, by the very nature of this operation, I want to be certain that none of you"—he looked directly at Jake Stock—"*none* of you has any reservations about what is to be done. So if anyone wants out, just say so now, and you will be replaced—no questions asked."

He paused, and Jake Stock glanced down at his own big hands resting on the table's edge. He knew no one would want out. It was a big deal—a chance to be a hero. He was the only one who wanted out, and Tolliver knew that —but Tolliver also knew that Stock would say nothing. A hatred for Tolliver was building within Stock, and he no longer tried to hold it back. It might be the only thing which would carry him through this whole crazy business.

"Good!" Tolliver slapped his hands together sharply. "Now, let me say one thing more. Once you leave the *Mudskipper* tonight, Lieutenant Stock here is in absolute command. That condition holds until you are back aboard. I don't have to impress on you the necessity for total discipline in an operation of this sort. The area has been checked out, and Lieutenant Stock will brief you on what you can expect to find when you get ashore. There is little chance that you will encounter anything out of the ordinary, but we have to assume that you may. I promise you one thing. When you come back, the *Mudskipper* will be there waiting for you. No matter what happens, we will be there!"

He paused to let that reassurance sink in. The man is good, Jake Stock admitted grudgingly. He could send you into hell itself and make it sound like a favor.

"One other thing," Tolliver said, and he sought out Stock's eyes, held them for a moment, and then turned his attention to the other men. "I came across some information which seems rather appropriate. It undoubtedly seems strange to some of you"—here again he glanced briefly at Stock—"that a submarine should go after a target on dry land. A submarine's home is the sea, under the sea. Its victims are sought in that natural habitat. Right?"

He was obviously enjoying himself—like a teacher, Stock thought, giving a lecture to a class.

"So, we plan to leave our natural habitat and seek a victim on dry land. A strange thing to do? Perhaps for any other submarine"—he smiled as though at some secret joke—"but not for this one. We're all a part of a sub called the *Mudskipper*. We know that the mudskipper is a fish, but how many of you know what kind of fish it is? I must confess I didn't know—not until a little while ago. I got out the dictionary—just on an impulse—and I turned to find *mudskipper* in it." He picked up a thick book from the wardroom table and opened it. Then, after a glance at Jake Stock, he read slowly: "Mudskipper. Any of several small Asiatic and Polynesian gobies which are able to leave the water and skip about actively over wet mud and sand and even to climb over the roots of mangroves in pursuit of their prey." He closed the book and looked up.

"So there you are. For any other sub, going ashore after a train might be foolish, but not for the *Mudskipper*. Because that's what a mudskipper does. He leaves the sea and goes up on the land *in pursuit of his prey*."

Once more his eyes challenged and mocked Jake Stock. Then he slapped his hands together and leaned back in his chair. "End of lesson. All right, Jake, they're all yours."

The eyes of the men at the table turned now to consider Stock. He tried to evaluate their opinion of him. He already knew how he stood with Amos Kenestrick. John Barringer was a loner, belonging to no cliques aboard the *Mudskipper*, and he would probably go along with Stock as well as with anyone.

Weslowski and Schroeder were Kenestrick's boys. They had already formed their opinion of Jake Stock, based on Kenestrick's undoubtedly vocal dislike for him. Stock had selected both men, knowing this to be the case, because he also knew they were best suited for the job. Tommy Lyle was a steady kid, a capable electrician and well liked by the rest of the crew. He would give no trouble. The biggest risk was Finley Tatum. He was erratic, given to drinking too much and getting in all sorts of trouble when he was ashore. Stock had handed out disciplinary punishment to him several times when the *Mudskipper* was in port. Once at sea, Tatum withdrew pretty much to himself, was moody, but otherwise caused no trouble. He had been busted in rank at least three times since Stock had known him, but it had always been for something that happened during a liberty. The fact remained that Tatum was probably the best night lookout on the *Mudskipper*, and this was why he had been selected. It remained to be seen whether the fact of dry land under his feet, even the

133

dry land of an enemy coast, would bring out the worst in him.

It's not a bad group, Stock thought. They might wish for better than me, but I'm satisfied with them.

"Okay," he said, painfully conscious of his own inadequacies as a speaker—particularly uncomfortable in the role of an officer speaking to these men, most of whom he had served with as an enlisted man. "What I have to say won't take long. We shouldn't have too much trouble getting in, although the boat'll be carrying a lot more load than it was last night. There isn't much beach there. The water comes right in to rocks that go up maybe ten to fifteen feet. Baldwin and I managed to find a place at the base of those rocks where we could store the boat, but I guess that depends on how lucky we are, whether we can do that tonight. It's possible we may have to haul it up to the top and leave it there.

"Schroeder and Tatum will stay with the boat. The main thing you guys have to watch out for is that you don't get trigger happy and start shooting at us when we come back. As far as we could tell last night, there isn't much chance we'll run into anyone, but that was last night and tonight could be different. If we're lucky, we'll have fog again tonight. It's easy to hide in the fog. Every man will carry a flashlight with the glass painted red. Any light you see that isn't red means trouble. Remember that."

Fritz Schroeder asked, "How long do you figure it'll take, Mr. Stock?"

"I would guess no more than an hour to get from where we leave the boat to the tracks, place the charge, and get back to the boat."

"Suppose you can't make it back in an hour," Finley

Tatum asked, "how long do we wait before—well, before . . ."

"Before you start to worry?" Stock asked. Tatum nodded. "Well, let's put it this way. If we're not back in an hour, then probably something has gone wrong—maybe with the bomb, maybe something else. Give us another fifteen minutes. If we don't show by then, one of you—you, Schroeder, come in and look for us. Come in quickly and quietly. Come as far as the tracks and that's all. If you don't find us, get the hell back."

Tolliver broke in. "Jake, you're supposing something that couldn't happen."

He wanted to tell Tolliver that anything could happen in a crazy deal like this, but instead he said, "Just trying to think of the worst that could happen, Captain. It's dark out there, and it's a strange and unfriendly place. The only way to make it work is to have a set of rules we play by, no matter what happens." He turned back to Tatum. "Does that answer your question? If we don't show in an hour and fifteen minutes, make a limited effort to find out what's wrong, then you and Schroeder get the hell out of there."

For the first time the men at the table were beginning to look concerned.

"Okay," Stock said, pleased in spite of himself that he had been able to shake them up a little. "Now to the rest of us. Lyle and Weslowski, you carry the bomb. We'll rig it in a sling and you can carry it between you. The sling'll come in handy for getting up those rocks, too. I don't have to tell you how important it is for you to keep your footing. It's dark, and the going is pretty rough. I'll be in front. Then you two with the bomb, and Barringer and the Chief will bring up the rear. If we can hit at around the same place we did last night, it'd be good. As far as Baldwin and I could tell the country is deserted in that vicinity. Baldwin spotted some sort of buildings a good ways up the tracks and off quite a way from the tracks. Of course, it's possible we missed seeing some things because of the fog."

Tolliver stirred restlessly. "You noted the time the train passed there last night, didn't you, Jake?"

"Yes, sir. When I checked after it passed me, the time was twenty-three twenty."

"Then you'll want to allow for its being a little earlier than that, just to be on the safe side—say half an hour?"

Stock nodded. "That ought to be plenty."

"Good. We'll allow an hour and fifteen minutes to get ashore, another hour and fifteen minutes to place the bomb and get back to the rubber boat. That's two and a half hours, and it should all be done by twenty-two fifty —right?"

Stock drew a deep breath and nodded. "Yes, sir."

Tolliver turned to Wes Clayton. "That means we'll want to be in launching position and have that boat ready by"—he made some notations on a pad of paper—"twenty fifteen. It should be dark enough by then, shouldn't it?"

Clayton nodded. "Just barely, Captain. Sun sets at nineteen forty-seven. It's clearing up out there today, so we won't know about the weather tonight. If there's fog again, fine, but if not we're due to have a full moon."

Tolliver smiled. "That ought to make for a very beautiful night. We'll have the fog, though. This time of year there's fog almost every night around here."

"Captain," Stock said, "if anything goes wrong tonight —if we run into anything, the decision to call it off is mine—right?"

This was not a question he had planned to ask. It was not, he knew, the proper time or place to ask it, because it placed Tolliver in an awkward position. He had given Stock complete authority already and now Stock was making him spell it out—not only as concerned the successful completion of the mission but also the possible abortion of the entire operation. In a way it was a challenge, and the sudden glint in Tolliver's eyes indicated that he recognized it as such.

Finally he replied. "In the event, Jake—in the highly unlikely event that anything should go wrong—yes, you have the authority to call it off."

He had a way of saying things, Stock thought with some bitterness, that makes him the winner in that exchange. For the way in which he had answered Stock said more than the words which were spoken—much more. It said, "Nothing will go that wrong, Jake. And if it does, then I will hold you personally responsible."

There was little else to be accomplished at that time. A few details were worked out. It was agreed that the men in the landing party should turn in and try to sleep for a couple of hours, eat at eighteen thirty and hold a last-minute briefing session at nineteen thirty. Night adaptation would commence at mealtime. Jake Stock, Amos Kenestrick, John Barringer, and Tommy Lyle were to get on immediately with the final work on the demolition package.

It was, Stock admitted to himself as he prepared to leave the wardroom, a good setup. There was no reason why it should not go well. The odds were against their running into any unexpected difficulties ashore. The bomb would work. Kenestrick knew what he was doing. The whole damned thing was going to be easy—too easy.

They would go ashore, place the bomb, get away, and the train would be destroyed. It would give the crew a big boost, make Tolliver happy, look good on the record, and make a hell of a war story to tell his son some day in the future.

Why then did he feel the way he did? He had tried to understand himself, and the reasons he had given himself were varied. The train was not worth the risk. The train was to be destroyed merely to satisfy a whim of Jonathan Tolliver. It was not the proper function of a submarine to play commando without the training for such an operation. There were answers to all these objections—good answers. But still the feeling persisted.

The real answer, he knew, lay deeper than that. It lay within Jake Stock, and it lay within Jonathan Tolliver— and Stock could no more identify that answer than he could rid himself of the growing sense of evil which surrounded the operation he was about to carry out for Tolliver.

Eleven

⚓

THE SOLDIER KOJIMA had spent most of his off-duty time in Kushiro wandering through the streets of the city. This was unusual for him. Ordinarily, once he had checked to see if the freight cars were properly unloaded, he would find some corner in the station and try to sleep until the time came to start preparations for the return trip to Nemuro. On this particular day, however, he had felt restless and so he had gone out, away from the railroad station. He had walked for several hours through the strange and crowded streets, looking into shops, watching people —and thinking.

He could not understand the mood which was upon him. The conversation he had had with the officer back in Nemuro that morning had disturbed him, of course—had intensified his own feeling of insignificance with the officer's boasting about the glories of battle. Kojima had never thought of himself as a soldier, had never aspired to be a soldier, but now he felt ashamed somehow.

Also he was worried about his daughter. Last night she had felt ill, had been feverish. She was very precious to him. His infant son, of course, should have a place of superior importance to a daughter, but his daughter was the one who came to him and took his hand in hers and looked up at him with great solemn eyes which told him of her trust and love. The infant son was not yet able to make this kind of overt indication of love.

As he walked the streets of the city, Kojima decided that he wanted to take his daughter something that night —something special, something he would purchase with the little money he had. It should be a thing which would have meaning for her alone. It should be a thing which would show her in a very special way that he loved her, because it was difficult for Kojima to say the words which could tell her this.

So he went into shops and searched for the proper gift, and finally he found a doll. It was not a large or a grand doll, but it possessed a quality—an expression on its painted face which reminded Kojima of his daughter. Somehow, as he looked at it, it seemed to be trying to tell him that it was the proper gift, the special gift for which he had been searching. It took all of the money he had with him, and he knew that his wife would scold him for spending the money on a doll, but his wife was in Nemuro and he was in Kushiro, and she could not stop him. He would endure his scolding which would not be really harsh, because she would understand why he had bought the doll. It was small enough to be carried inside his jacket, and its very presence close to his body made him feel better. Soon after he had purchased it, he returned to the railway station and waited there until it was time to begin loading the train.

As he waited, he took the doll from his jacket and held it in his hands, watching the painted face carefully, seeing his daughter's face, imagining the way her eyes would widen with joy when she too saw the doll and understood that it was hers—that her father had brought it especially for her all the way from the great city of Kushiro. And, sitting on the station floor, holding the doll, Kojima felt strangely at peace with himself and with the world in which he lived. It was of no importance that he was a simple man, a soldier who had never known battle, a person of no consequence. He lived. He loved and was loved. The violence of war would perhaps pass him by completely and he would be permitted to go on living and loving. He would watch his daughter grow into a woman, and his son into a man, and they would honor him as their father. It would not matter to them that he was not a brave warrior. There would be other things in their world which would have importance, and Kojima would grow old with dignity and peace, knowing the great joy of children. And one day, when his daughter had a daughter of her own, perhaps she would give her daughter this very doll and tell her of the time it had been given to her. It would be the first doll she had received, and it would be forever precious and important.

And in that time, when he sat and held the doll, Kojima knew a great happiness.

"There she is!"

Amos Kenestrick stepped back and looked admiringly at the bomb. It rested on the deck of the after torpedo room, a squat boxlike contraption, heavily wrapped in black oilskin and secured with metal bands. Kenestrick bent over and carefully lifted it a few inches from the deck, grunting with the effort.

"Jeez, this thing is heavier than it looks. Must be about sixty-five pounds."

Jake Stock studied the bomb. It looked strangely harmless, he thought—such a neatly wrapped package. As a boy in high school, he had worked one Christmas for a local department store, delivering parcels. Hour after hour he would race from the delivery truck up to houses to ring or knock and hand people packages which were destined to be a part of that joyous season. This looked just like one of those packages—neat and mysterious—its contents disguised by the wrapping. There was a difference, though. The Christmas packages he had delivered had been wrapped in gaily colored paper, and their mysteries were meant to bring joy. This package which he was to deliver on a strange shore was wrapped in black, and it contained only horror and death.

"Where do you make the connections for the detonator?"

Kenestrick replaced the bomb on the deck and knelt to pull away a double thickness of black tape at one corner. "The leads are right in here. I'm keeping it taped over until we get it there to keep out any water. We'll have to make the connections on the spot, but that shouldn't take long."

The Electrician's Mate, John Barringer, was perched on the edge of a bunk, listening. He said, "Say, Chief, I've been thinking maybe we ought to use two switches, one on each rail. I mean, we could wire in the two of them about as easy as one, and that way we'd be protected against something going wrong with one of them."

Kenestrick nodded enthusiastically. "Yeah! That's good, John, real good. How about the size of the terminals in there? Will you need to enlarge them to handle the two switches?"

"I don't think so. Here, I'll check it out. Let me get some more wire."

Stock wanted to leave. There was nothing for him to do here. The thing was already in motion, and nothing he could do would stop it. The important thing, he thought, is to get it done. Never mind what I am doing or why. Go in and do it and get out . . .

"I'll be in my quarters, Amos."

Kenestrick glanced up with a grin. "Going to catch some sack time? That's not a bad idea."

"I'll check with you before I eat, Amos."

Kenestrick was already back at the bomb, his back turned to Stock. "Yeah, Lieutenant, see you then . . ."

When Stock reached his quarters he found Tom Friday stretched out on the top bunk. The Engineering Officer was reading, and when Stock entered he closed the book and sat up, swinging his long legs over the side of the bunk.

"Hi, Jake. I guess you'll be wanting to catch a little sack time. I can clear out of here."

He liked Friday, probably more than he did any of the other officers on the *Mudskipper*. For one thing, Friday made him feel less uncomfortable than the others. Friday was a Reserve, while all the other officers on the boat, with the exception of Stock, were Annapolis men. Tolliver was sticky about that. As the war had dragged on and submarine operations had become more and more extensive, it had been necessary to train an increasing number of Reserve officers for what had once been an almost completely elite branch of the Navy. There were even two or three Reserve officers in command of fleet submarines, but

Tolliver had fought tooth and nail to hold this incursion to a minimum on his boat. Tom Friday, for all his awkward, gangling appearance, was as good an engineering man as could be found in the service. A graduate of North Carolina State College, he looked as though he would be more at home behind a plow than in an officer's uniform, but he was the kind of man Tolliver could smell out and use. And Jake Stock, of course, was Tolliver's own creation. For the rest of the officers Tolliver had crack Annapolis men.

Stock and Friday were not close, despite the fact that they shared quarters, but they had a mutual respect for each other. Now, however, Jake Stock suddenly wanted to talk with Friday.

"Don't rush off, Tom. I'm going to stretch out for a while, but I don't figure on sleeping much. Stick around and cheer me up."

The Engineering Officer grinned broadly. "Come on, man, you're kidding me. Here you are getting ready to go off on something I'd give my eye teeth to be in on, and you want cheering up?"

Stock had removed his shoes, and he crawled into the lower bunk, stretching to his full length and trying to drive away the tightness in his neck and back. "You'd really like to be in on this, wouldn't you, Tom?"

"Hell, who wouldn't?" Coming from above, the other man's voice sounded hollow and faraway—unreal, Stock thought wearily. Like everything else in this crazy business—unreal. "I mean," Friday was saying, "you're in on something nobody else in this whole war has done—no submariner, that is. Real commando stuff—just like this movie I saw back home in Raleigh." He laughed softly at the memory. "It had Tyrone Power in it—and Dana Andrews. They were submarine officers in New London, and they were both in love with Anne Baxter. And then they got sent on this secret mission somewhere in the North Atlantic—some place like Iceland, only it wasn't Iceland. Anyway, the Nazis had this big oil-storage place there on this island, and Tyrone Power took a landing party ashore and blew the living hell out of the place.

"Man, that was really something. I mean, he was dressed all in black and had this black stuff smeared on his face so it'd be hard to see him at night, and they went in there and just lit up that Nazi oil-storage place like the Fourth of July."

Stock closed his eyes. "Did they get away?"

"Sure. Oh, of course, a couple of guys got killed—somebody like Alan Hale. You know, there're always a couple of the good guys you can count on getting killed. But old Tyrone Power made it out of there with those oil tanks exploding all around him, and he got back to the sub, and the next thing you know that sub was sailing into New London with a broom lashed to the mast and the band was playing and everybody a hero. I forget which one of them finally got Anne Baxter. I think it was probably Tyrone Power. Anyway, that movie was what made me decide I wanted to get into submarines." He chuckled. "That's a hell of a reason, isn't it?"

The tightness would not leave him. Stock willed himself to relax. It was all decided. There was nothing he could or would do now to stop the march of events. He could only make himself as ready for what was to come as possible, and this meant relaxing.

What had Tom said?

There're always a couple of the good guys you can count on getting killed.

"Why'd you pick out submarines, Jake?" Friday asked.

And where, Stock wondered, was the answer to that question?

It seemed so long ago.

"I don't know. It was back before we actually got into the war . . ."

Talking like this helped him to relax. His eyes remained closed, and he could hear his own voice, but it seemed to belong to someone else. "I joined up in thirty-nine, I guess it was. Yeah, thirty-nine. I was just out of high school, and I had a chance to go to college, but in thirty-nine I got the idea that war was coming, and I felt like I ought to be ready for whatever came along, so I enlisted. I was in boot camp at Great Lakes, and there was this Chief there, named Rufus Morgan. I'll never forget him. He'd been on the boats, and he used to talk a lot about them and what great duty it was. Most of all, though, I guess it was the kind of man Rufus was himself that decided me. I think I admired him more than any man I'd ever known, and I figured if a man like Rufus could come out of sub duty, then there must be something to be said for it. Anyway, when I was about ready to finish boot, I put in for New London—and I made it. I think Rufus had a lot to do with getting me into sub school."

"Do you know where he is now?" Friday asked.

"The last time I saw him, he was down in Key West. That was back in forty-two. I was in the States, and I put in a couple of weeks at the sub base down there. Old Rufus was instructor for a bunch of Reserve officers who were on their way to New London." Stock chuckled at the memory. "He was sitting out in front of a quonset, playing cribbage with another Chief and drinking black coffee by the gallon. He had more hashmarks on his sleeve than you've ever seen. I went over and told him who I was, and he was nice enough to pretend he remembered me. Anyway, there he was, drawing all that longevity and going out to make a dive on one of the R-boats once a month so he could draw sea pay and sub pay, and I'll bet he was making more money than an Admiral."

The tightness was almost gone. Perhaps, he thought sleepily, I am an old man like Rufus. I find peace in the past, thinking about the good old days. A game of cribbage and a cup of black coffee in the Florida sun—that is what I am good for now . . .

"Man oh man," Tom Friday was saying, "the way Hollywood makes it look so easy. There was this other movie I saw about a year ago—with Cary Grant in it. I saw it with a bunch of guys on the tender back in Midway, and we were laughing so hard you couldn't hear a damned thing. You see, in this one, Cary Grant is the skipper of this sub, and he decides to take his boat right into Tokyo Bay, only they have some crazy kind of antisubmarine nets guarding the entrance to Tokyo Bay, so Cary Grant waits around until this Jap ship comes along and they have to open the nets for the ship, so he puts his boat right up under the Jap, and they go in while the net is open . . ."

The voice faded and was gone, and Jake Stock hung suspended between sleeping and waking, the tensions gone, his body wonderfully light and free, floating in a black void. His mind was last to yield to sleep, shutting off Tom Friday's voice to concentrate on a startlingly clear image of Helen who was looking at him and smiling and nodding her head, her lips moving soundlessly, trying, he knew, to speak his name. He wanted to tell her it was all right, that he knew what she was trying to say. And then the smile was gone, and her face turned solemn, and he was able to see it close—so very close—until all he could see was one eye, one great, beautiful brown eye in which a tear was forming—quite tiny at first, then growing larger and larger until it filled the eye and spilled over.

But before he could discover why Helen had shed that tear, he was asleep.

Twelve

⚓

IT WAS LATE in the afternoon when Takeo made his great decision. It was not a suddenly arrived-at thing, although he was surprised at his own audacity once the decision was finally and irrevocably made. He had finished his work in the field, and he was very tired and very hungry as he lagged behind his grandfather on the way back to the house. All day his grandfather had been constantly scolding him for being slow in his work, despite the fact that Takeo did twice as much work as the old man. However, it was not this which decided him. He had been slow at his work that day, and it was understandable that the old man should have scolded him. Takeo respected his grandfather despite the fact that he was a quarrelsome old man and inclined to find fault easily. This decision had to do only with Takeo himself, and once it was made he felt filled with a new strength.

Waiting for his mother to finish preparing the evening meal, he made his plans. There were not many belongings which he would have need of. The clothing he wore would suffice. If it were possible, he would like to have the photograph of his father, but he knew that its place on the wall of the house was sacred and that his mother would need the picture to give her strength when he was gone. For a moment, the thought of leaving his mother with only his grandfather to care for her and give her company made him waver. But, he decided, it would not be forever. He would come back again when he was a man. He would return, and he could visualize that returning—a Takeo grown to be a man like his father, full of strength and courage and wisdom, coming to the door of his mother's house. She would open the door and see him, and she would smile—as he remembered her smiling in the past, and she would know joy for the rest of her life because her son would take care of her and protect her. For the time that he was gone, for the time it would take him to grow into a man, she must endure that which must be endured.

But he would not take his father's photograph with him. He must carry the likeness of his father in his mind and leave the photograph in its proper and sacred place on the wall. The one thing he would take, he decided, was the knife which had belonged to his father. His father had taken it with him when he went to sea for fish. It was a good knife with a handle of bone and a long, thin blade which Takeo's grandfather had taught him to keep sharp. He would take the knife, and that would serve to remind him of his father—only the knife and the clothing which he wore—and from that humble beginning, he would grow into a man.

And so Takeo waited for the night, waited for darkness to cover the land, waited for his mother and his grandfather to sleep, waited for the time when he would leave this house for the last time as a boy—when he would go out into the night to await the coming of the train and the man who would stop the train and take Takeo away with him to the world in which a boy could be transformed into a man.

Jonathan Tolliver had not slept during the past forty-eight hours. He was the only one who knew this. He had spent several hours stretched out on his bunk, with the stateroom dark, but he had not slept. His body had begged for rest, but his mind would not permit it. The thing, his mind said, is too near at hand to risk sleep. If the body is permitted to surrender to its weakness, then the thing may not be done. Sleep had become a danger, a trap.

And so he forced his will upon the weakness of his body, holding his mind under rigid control, concentrating on the train—on the mission. And, strangely enough, he seemed to grow stronger. He told himself that he had passed some critical point, beyond which his body could go indefinitely without sleep. It was an exhilarating thought—as though he had somehow become endowed with some power beyond the power of ordinary men.

The thing must be done. The train must be destroyed.

Over and over again, he fed his new strength with these pledges. He had overcome the problem of the Japanese ship which had threatened to intervene. Now, nothing could stop him.

And yet, all around the periphery of his seemingly invincible power to keep going, he was aware that an enemy lurked. The enemy was fatigue—massive, incredibly powerful, determined to seize upon the slightest sign of weakness on his part to move against him. Fatigue was a huge, shapeless presence of which he was constantly aware.

And once—only once—he thought he sensed the presence of another enemy—allied with fatigue—an enemy with the face of madness.

He made it into a game, to help him stay alert. It became a fine game, one which excited him as much as the object of the game itself—the train. The destruction of the train—by Jonathan Tolliver—this was the end of the game. No matter that Jake Stock was to be his instrument, his was the actual hand of destruction—and when that was accomplished, then he would have won the game. Then he could surrender his body to sleep and laugh at fatigue even as he gave himself up to it.

He looked at his watch. Shortly after seventeen hundred hours. Only a little over two hours until the sun would be setting, he thought, only that much more time in which anything could go wrong. Tolliver possessed a mystic confidence in the power of darkness. Once night came, then nothing could stop him.

Only one tangible obstacle remained in his way, and that was Jake Stock. He had not convinced Jake of the importance of the train, but he knew that Jake would not fail him. He had been trained too carefully. He would do the thing he was told to do, even if it cost him his life . . .

If Jake Stock should die, carrying out Tolliver's mission . . .

This was the thought he had not previously permitted himself to have. Now it had thrust itself upon him, and he could not escape it.

Jake Stock belonged to him—in the same way Adam had belonged to the God who had created him. Tolliver had taken the dust of nothingness and breathed life into it and shaped it and molded it and produced a man—a miracle of courage and skill at the game of war. Now that creation had questioned him. The thing Jake Stock had been before would never have dared dream of resisting Tolliver. He wondered if God had felt pride when his creation had dared to raise its voice in rebellion against Him . . .

His eyes closed, and for a moment he felt himself slipping away into the blackness of fatigue which laid siege to him. Desperately he fought his way back.

Jake Stock! He must concentrate on Jake Stock!

Of course, mixed with the pride, there was also anger and the absolute necessity for punishment. Punishment was the true mark of love. Jonathan Tolliver had been taught that lesson well by his father, a good man—a man who had a closeness with God. Yes, he had been taught that lesson so thoroughly that he would never forget it.

Leaving his stateroom, Jonathan Tolliver moved down the passageway. When he came to Jake Stock's quarters he stopped, pulled the curtain aside and looked inside. The big man was asleep. Tolliver could just make out his face in the semidarkness. Sleep was no problem for Stock, he thought. He was like a child, and children could sleep under any circumstances. And, because they could sleep, they became helpless. Nothing, Tolliver thought, is more helpless than a sleeping child.

The sleeping man-child who was Jake Stock stirred, and Tolliver froze, hardly daring to breathe. Then Stock was still again, and on his lips there was now a smile. The dreams of children are happy, Tolliver thought with a sudden bitterness, and eventually the child must pay the price for those happy dreams.

153

He did love Jake Stock. Watching the big man sleeping there, his face a child's face, relaxed and smiling, Tolliver's heart filled with love for him, with compassion and understanding.

Sleep soundly, he thought. Sleep and dream your happy child's dreams. For a few minutes more you can belong to that world. Then you must return to my world and face me and go out to do the thing I have willed you to do— *for me*. And I will love you for doing my will and hate you because I want to do it with my own hand, not yours. You will destroy the train for me.

Once again, the darkness of his own monumental weariness threatened to engulf him, and the wild, desperate, unreasoning thoughts swirled in his mind.

If Jake Stock should die . . .

Thirteen

⚓

Tomiji, the fireman on Inouye's train, had spent his off-duty hours in Kushiro in his usual way, which is to say he had been drinking and gambling. Tomiji's life was sharply divided into two parts. For approximately twenty hours of the twenty-four in each day, he was a miserable and abject slave to the two persons who ruled him with hands and wills of iron. One was Inouye. The other was his wife. Mercifully, the more unbearable of these two tyrants, his wife, had less chance to torment him than did Inouye. All that Inouye demanded of him was constant, back-breaking labor to keep the firebox supplied with coal, to keep the locomotive gleaming. His wife's tongue was far more oppressive than Inouye's dictatorial silence. But he was with her only for a few hours each night, and he could usually escape her scolding voice by falling asleep, although he was certain that she continued to rail at him long after he had been mercifully delivered from her by unconsciousness, for when he awakened in the darkness of

155

the early morning, she would be talking, and for all he knew she had been talking all through the time he slept.

But each afternoon, for a few precious hours while he was free from duty in the city of Kushiro, Tomiji would go to the place of Mr. Sato, who was the very good friend of anyone with a few coins to spend. There he would sit with the other men and drink great quantities of *awamori* and play at *Mah Jong*, generally losing the little money which he had, but on rare and wonderful afternoons winning a little so that he could buy more *awamori*. Actually, it did not matter to Tomiji whether he won or lost at Mr. Sato's. Money had little meaning for him. Any money he managed to hold on to would be taken from him by his wife and used to buy food for her and their six children. Once his wife had been young and submissive. He had known how to still her tongue then, but she had grown old and fat and angry, and now Tomiji feared and hated her.

The joy of those afternoons spent at the place of Mr. Sato did not depend on winning at *Mah Jong*. Those afternoons were the escape which Tomiji needed so desperately from that other world. During those hours no man and no woman stood over him telling him what he must do and when he must do it. The men who gathered at Mr. Sato's were much like Tomiji himself. They talked little, drank as much as possible, and played at *Mah Jong* with a desperate and consuming joy.

On this particular afternoon Tomiji had been very lucky. He had won more money than at any time he could remember, and, as a result, he had broken one of his self-imposed rules. It would be a madness to report back for duty on Inouye's train in a drunken state, and so Tomiji had learned to drink just enough and no more. He was always able, by plunging his head into a basin of cold water several times and walking the distance from Mr. Sato's place to the railroad station to be reasonably sober by the time he reached the locomotive. On this afternoon, however, he was so overwhelmed by his luck that he had ordered a full extra bottle of *awamori* and drunk practically all of it himself. As a result he had lost track of the time, so that by the time he realized what was happening, he knew he would be late. Frantically, still dazed with too much drink, Tomiji gathered what he could find of his belongings and, cursing Inouye, his wife, and the world in general, stumbled out of Mr. Sato's place and started to run toward the station.

"Mr. Stock . . ."

The hand touched his shoulder gently, and for a moment he thought it must be Helen's hand, so he smiled, still half asleep, and turned to face her.

"Mr. Stock, it's time to get up. The Captain told me to get you."

As his eyes opened they saw the brown face of Roy Watson. The Steward's Mate was bending over him in the darkened room.

"You awake now, Mr. Stock?"

"Yeah, Roy. I'm awake."

"I brought you in some coffee. It's on the desk there."

"Thanks, Roy."

Watson moved to the doorway, then looked back at Stock, who still lay on his bunk. "You sure you're awake, Mr. Stock?"

He could hear his mother's voice coming up from the kitchen which was directly under his room. Each morning she would tap on the kitchen ceiling with the end of the broom and call him at six-thirty to get up and get ready for school, and he would answer her and think he could steal a few more minutes in the warmth of his bed, but in another minute the broom would tap again, and she would call, "Are you awake, Jake?" And he would answer that he was awake, but that would not satisfy her. "Are you out of bed, Jake?" And that would mean he had actually to put his feet on the floor and get out of bed. Helen was not that way. When he was with Helen she would get up and prepare his breakfast and bring it to him while he was still in bed, and she would sit on the edge of the bed and watch him eat.

He swung his feet from the bunk and put them on the deck. "There, Roy. That okay?"

Watson grinned. "Yessir. The Captain says he wants you in the wardroom in ten minutes."

Stock reached for the mug of coffee and sat on the edge of the bunk sipping the scalding-hot liquid. The memory of sleep was relinquished with great reluctance. He had been dreaming, but he could not remember the subject of the dream or, indeed, anything of the dream other than the fact that it had been a pleasant one. It had undoubtedly been of Helen, he decided, since she was usually the subject of his dreams. He could remember a book from which his mother had read to him when he was very small—a love story about two people who loved each other very much, but for many reasons were unable to be together. They had devised a way of dreaming together —of creating a special world which they could share. They had called it "dreaming true." That was all Jake Stock could remember of the book. He could not recall its title or who had written it, and he knew that his mother had read it not to him but for herself. She worked so hard and had so little time that she could not justify reading for her own entertainment, so she read the books she wanted to read aloud to her son. Jake Stock understood now what the wonder of that book's "dreaming true" must have meant to his widowed mother. Once, when he was home on leave with Helen, he had wanted to tell her about the book, to tell her how wonderful it would be if they could find some way of creating a life together in their dreams during the long months they were apart. But he lacked the ability to express thoughts like that with words, so he had said nothing.

Still, he thought, in a way we do have a dream life together. A Helen in a dream had more reality than most of the things which happened in the waking world. She was certainly more real than a train that ran along tracks on a strange shore . . .

And that brought him back to the waking world, to the reality which was not real. Then the thought struck him with such force that he rose to his feet, startled and frightened. If he were to be killed on Tolliver's mission, then he had slept and dreamed for the last time. In Jake Stock's mind there was no romantic notion about death. He did not equate it with eternal sleep. It was a stopping of life, an end to all things. His unknown father did not await Jake Stock in some paradise. When death came, when the air had given out in that caved-in mine, that had been all. There had been only blackness then—no spiritual survival to await a reunion with his wife, to see his unborn son. For the man whose seed had helped create the flesh which was Jake Stock there had been nothing more. And if Jake Stock met death on that strange shore this night, there would be nothing more for him—no sleep in which there were dreams of Helen. And so, if he had dreamed of her, it might have been his goodbye to her. And that, he thought, was as it should be. There would be no time for goodbyes past this point. He did not want to die. He did not intend to die, but the knowledge of the possibility of death was so strong upon him that he could not ignore it.

In that dream, then, he had said his goodbye. Perhaps, wherever she was, Helen had shared his dream. Perhaps the wonder and magic of the old story his mother had read him had worked that one time. It was a thought which gave him strength, and he seized on it and held to it and came to believe it.

He finished the coffee, ran cold water into the wash basin and bent over it, scooping up handfuls and dipping his face into them. The time for dreaming was past.

He found Tolliver awaiting him in the wardroom, and he was mildly surprised to note the tight lines of fatigue on the Commanding Officer's face. Tolliver as a mere creature of flesh and blood and subject to strain was a new discovery for Stock.

"Hello, Jake." His voice sounded tired and uncertain. "Did you get a good rest?"

Stock nodded. "Yes, sir. I slept awhile."

Tolliver laughed briefly. "I know. I looked in on you. You were sleeping like a baby."

He did not know why the thought of Tolliver's watching him sleep disturbed him. It seemed somehow an invasion of privacy—the viewing of a secret and personal part of himself. It was, he thought, almost as though Tolliver had the power to see not only the man as he slept, but also within the man—to see his dreams. He did not want Jonathan Tolliver invading that world of his.

Tolliver's fingers were tapping restlessly on the table's edge. "It's a little before eighteen hundred, Jake. I told Roy to have you something to eat in a few minutes. He's fixing you a nice steak."

Stock grinned bleakly. "A hearty meal, Captain?"

Tolliver stared at him curiously for a moment, then nodded. "Sure, Jake. Why not?"

"For the condemned man?" He asked the question without anger. Just for an instant, Tolliver's mask cracked, and he seemed about to explode. Then, with an obvious effort, his face relaxed. The man's control was giving way, Stock realized, and for the first time he was beginning to understand Jonathan Tolliver.

"Condemned man, Jake? Don't be a damned fool. What do the British call it—a piece of cake? That's what it is, Jake, a piece of cake."

"Sure," Stock said. "I guess you're right, Captain."

The moment had passed. He had seen Tolliver start to slip, and he had helped him avoid it. That was the way it had to be.

Now Tolliver slapped his hands together with a laugh. He was all right again. "I'll tell Roy to get your steak ready now, Jake, and we can talk while you eat. That'll give you time to get into your commando suit in plenty of time to meet with the rest of the landing party."

Is there anything special we have to talk about, Captain? I mean, any last-minute change of plans?"

Tolliver considered him for several seconds before replying. Then he smiled and shook his head. "No, Jake. The *Mudskipper* will leave the sea and seek its prey on the land. It's as simple as that. There's nothing new—no changes." His eyes clouded for a moment, and he glanced down at his hands, then murmured, "I just thought—we could talk . . ."

It was a plea.

Fourteen

⚓

WHEN KURITA had first been issued the rifle, he had taken great pains to see that it was always kept in the best possible condition. He would spend many hours cleaning and oiling the rifle, for it was indeed a mark of distinction and rank that he alone of all the men in the patrol was trusted to carry such a weapon. Of late, however, he had become lax and careless with the rifle. It was, after all, a great deal of trouble to take it apart and clean it. There was no one who inspected it—no one who really cared whether it was clean and oiled or not, and so Kurita had gradually lessened his attention to its maintenance. At first he would allow a day or so to pass between cleanings—then a week, two weeks, and now he could not remember the last time he had disassembled the weapon for cleaning and oiling.

It would be difficult to know what prompted him to resume his maintenance late on this afternoon. He had been thinking a great deal about his interview with the officer that morning. The mere fact that a small part of the great war had indeed taken place so near to the coast where Kurita and his men patrolled had made an impression on him. More than that, however, there was the feeling which persisted that there had been something alien— something of danger in the darkness of the previous night —something which somehow was related to the war of which Kurita was such a small and insignificant part. Whatever the reason, on this afternoon, when the sun was beginning to sink toward the horizon, the old man took down his rifle and placed it carefully on some rags he had spread on the floor for that purpose. Then, squatting beside the rags, he carefully took the rifle apart as he had been taught. It was a bolt-action model which took a clip of six shells. With great pains he wiped all of the metal parts with an oily rag, taking great care with the swabbing out of the inside of the barrel. When he was satisfied that it was thoroughly cleaned, he reassembled it, proud of his ability to perform such a complex task. Then he held it up, nestled the stock in the hollow of his bony shoulder, and sighted along the barrel. He had never actually fired the rifle, even in practice. His left arm trembled with the weight of the weapon. His finger curled around the trigger and pulled. There was a loud click, but Kurita imagined the sudden, frightening roar of the rifle—imagined the death scream of a man he did not know as the powerful bullet ripped into his flesh, tearing the life from his body. In his entire life Kurita had never taken the life of another man. He had never seen a man die violently. But with this weapon of destruction, the mere movement of one finger could kill a man.

It was a thought which excited and frightened Kurita, and, as he lowered the rifle, he was trembling with more than the weight of the weapon. He remembered the story of the officer—of how the pilot had dropped his bombs on the hated American submarine and totally destroyed it. What must that brave pilot have felt, knowing that he had accomplished the death of many men. Of course the pilot could not see those men die. This was to Kurita a mysterious thing—that one could attack and kill men and never, never actually see them. With his weapon—with this carefully cleaned and well-oiled rifle he held in his hands —he would be able to see a man, to take aim at the man and take in the full view of him—and see him as the bullet tore through his flesh—see him fall—watch the blood run out of him.

And, lost in the wonder and terror of such thoughts, Kurita put the rifle aside and ate his simple meal in preparation for the long night which was ahead of him.

Amos Kenestrick had slept only a short while when he awoke with the pain knotting his side. When it grew more severe, he was forced to call for the *Mudskipper*'s Pharmacist's Mate, Donny Packard. Packard examined him carefully, probing and poking at the tender area on the lower right abdomen. Then he made his way forward to the wardroom with the word that, according to his diagnosis, Kenestrick was suffering from an attack of appendicitis—just how severe an attack Packard would not be able to tell for several hours.

By this time Wes Clayton had joined Tolliver and Jake Stock in the wardroom. Stock had just finished his steak when Packard came in with the news.

Tolliver listened, sat quietly for a moment, then asked, "What if he needs an operation?"

Packard looked uncomfortable. "I don't know, Captain. I don't think it's that bad yet. Sometimes a guy will have a

164

flareup and get over it with no trouble. I wouldn't even swear right now that it is the appendix, but that's the best guess I can make."

"Then your suggestion is that we wait and see what develops?"

"Yes, sir." Packard shifted nervously for a moment, then added, "Of course, he's out as far as the landing party is concerned."

Tolliver shot a quick glance at Jake Stock. The big man was watching him, his face expressionless. "Yes, of course. All right, Packard. Keep him quiet and let me know if there's any change."

"Yes, sir." Packard turned and left the wardroom.

Tolliver's fingers drummed relentlessly on the edge of the table. "Jake, what does this do to things?"

"I don't know, Captain. Amos knows more about the bomb than anyone, of course, seeing as how he put it together."

"But you can handle it, Jake?"

Stock nodded. "Yes, sir. I suppose I can."

"I wanted you to concern yourself with the overall operation. If you're going to have to be working directly with the bomb . . ."

Wes Clayton stirred. "Captain, let me go in with them."

"No!" Tolliver held up one hand. The idea had been with him all along, but he had forced himself to reject it. Now it had been forced back upon him, and he liked it. He liked it very much. A fresh excitement was building within him. "I'll do what I should have done from the first."

"What's that, Captain?" Clayton asked.

He smiled at the Executive Officer. "Simple, Wes. I'm

going to lead the landing party myself."

"What!" Stock half rose from his seat.

"You heard me, Jake. I'm going ashore with you. I should have done it all along. It was my idea. I planned it. You don't really have much stomach for it anyway, Jake, so that's the way it's going to be." He turned to Clayton. "Wes, you'll assume command of the *Mudskipper* while I am gone."

"Captain, you're not serious!" Clayton looked to Jake Stock for support. "You can't risk your neck like that!"

"Can't I?" Tolliver's expression hardened. He was beginning to suspect now that Clayton was against him as well as Stock. "As Commanding Officer of the *Mudskipper*, I can do anything I want, Wes—as long as it is not counter to Navy Regulations."

"But, Captain—"

"Isn't that right, Jake?" Tolliver cut the Executive Officer off curtly. "Or do you agree with Wes?"

Stock leaned back with an odd smile. "You're the Captain."

Tolliver stared at him suspiciously, then smiled. "That's right, Jake. I'm glad you see it that way." He slapped his hands together lightly. "All right, that's settled. I will assume command of the landing party. Jake, from now on, the bomb is your responsibility."

"Aye, aye, Captain." Stock started to rise.

"And, Jake," Tolliver said, "the responsibility for determining whether the mission is carried out naturally falls on me."

Stock looked at him and nodded slowly. "Naturally, Captain."

"But I can't imagine any reason why it should not be carried out, can you, Jake?"

166

"No, sir."

"No—no reason at all." Tolliver rose. "Wes, let's go to my stateroom and go over some things. Jake, you'll want to check in with Kenestrick, won't you?"

"Yes, sir. I'm on my way there now."

"Good. Tell him I'll stop by in a little while. Make sure he's comfortable."

As Stock made his way aft, he was torn by conflicting emotions about this sudden development. It was only fair that Tolliver should go along. After all, it was his crazy idea, and if anyone's neck was going to be stuck out, his should be. At the same time he dreaded the thought of having Tolliver with him. There was something wrong with the man, something Stock could not understand though he sensed it so strongly that he had come to dread being near him. It was as though whatever had infected Tolliver might somehow be communicated to those around him. The mission itself was touched with that infection, but now its source would become an integral part of the mission. Stock's chief hope had been that somehow, once he was clear of the *Mudskipper*, he might be able to bring some semblance of sanity to the carrying out of the operation. If he could manage to get the thing done and still escape from the dark and frightening *reasons* for it, then there was hope for him. With Jonathan Tolliver going along, he knew he would not be able to escape those reasons, for they were within Tolliver.

Amos Kenestrick had been bedded down in the after torpedo room. His face looked thinner and more drawn than usual, and his color was bad. Stock stood beside him.

"How's it going, Amos?"

Kenestrick forced a grin. "You bum," he whispered. "Of

167

all the lousy damned luck."

"One of those things, Amos. Don't sweat it."

"Look, Jake, there're a couple of things I want to say."
He winced suddenly.

"Take it easy, Amos."

"How else can I take it?"

"Have you been having any trouble before?"

"No. It'll be okay. If you think I'm going to get myself
in a place where that damned Pharmacist's Mate gets a
chance to be a hero and cut into my gut, forget it. Look,
Jake—I just wanted you to know I wish I was going
ashore with you, that's all. I mean, I've been sore ever
since the old man pinned those bars on you instead of me,
but you're the guy who ought to have them. I knew that
all along, but I was too damned stubborn to admit it."

Stock was aware of the sudden moisture in his own
eyes, and he welcomed it. "Thanks, Amos. I wish you
were going along too. I could sure as hell use you."

"You bet you could. Who's taking my place—as if anybody could."

"I am."

"You? I know you're going. I mean, isn't anyone filling
in for me? I thought the old man was dead set on having
seven men."

"He is. Like I said, I'm filling in for you, and the Captain is filling in for me."

There was a long silence. Then Kenestrick whistled
softly. "He must be off his rocker!"

Stock grinned bleakly. "You wouldn't want to put that
in writing, would you, Amos?"

Kenestrick had struggled to a sitting position. His shock
and concern were genuine. "I mean, Jake, he's the skipper
of this damned boat. The Captain isn't supposed to go off

on some crazy landing-party deal . . ."

"I thought you were all for this, Amos."

"I was. I am, but that's not the point. I mean, it's a great idea to go in and blow up that train. Those Japs'll never figure it out, and nobody but the old man could think up something like that. But having him go along and risk his neck is something else. You tried to talk him out of it, didn't you?"

Stock shook his head. "No. He's the man. If he says he's going, then he goes."

"But—" Another stab of pain sent Kenestrick back on the bunk. For a moment he lay there, his face contorted until the spasm had passed. "Damn!"

"You want me to call Packard?"

"No! It'll be okay. I saw the way that kid was looking at me. He read where some Pharmacist's Mate got a medal for cutting some poor guy's appendix out, and he's just sharpening his knife, hoping he'll get a crack at mine. Fat chance!'

"Packard's a good man, Amos. If it came to the worse, he could do it."

"Never mind about me and my appendix. I'm worried about the skipper going with you."

"He means a lot to you, doesn't he, Amos?"

"What kind of question is that? Yeah, he means a lot to me, and he should to you too. We've been through some things with that guy, Jake. There's not a skipper in the whole damned fleet that can stand up to him. There're not many guys in this world that I'd say was worth dying for, but in my book, he's one of them."

For a moment Stock did not say anything. There was no point in arguing with Kenestrick. He needed to be quiet and free from worry.

"It'll be okay, Amos. He's set on going, and that's that."

"Look, Jake, take care of him."

Stock took a deep breath. "Yeah, Amos, I'll do my best. Now look, there're a couple of things I want to check out on that bomb of yours . . ."

And as they talked, Stock felt the chilling mantle of a new responsibility settling upon him. Amos Kenestrick had not placed it there. Amos had merely put it into words. Jake Stock had known of it from the moment Jonathan Tolliver had announced that he was going ashore with the landing party. It was a responsibility which transcended all others—even the safeguarding of his own life.

He had the responsibility of keeping a god safe from harm—a god, he suspected, who was cracking, but nevertheless a god.

Fifteen

⚓

THE SOLDIER KOJIMA watched as the last crates were loaded aboard the freight car. Once the workmen were clear, he pulled himself up into the car and made his routine inspection, checking the several crates and cartons against his copy of the loading list. Less than a third of the car was being used, and the car just behind this one was completely empty. Kushiro, he thought, received far more from the little village of Nemuro than it gave in return. It did not surprise him. The great always took more from the weak than they gave back. This undoubtedly explained their greatness.

When he had finished checking the car, he walked along the station platform, beyond the covered portion, and found a grassy spot where he sat to await the time for the train's departure. The sun was very low in the sky. It was going to be a clear night, Kojima thought. Unless the fog came in, it would be very beautiful. He decided to ride in the empty freight car at the end of the train on the return trip. By leaving the door partially open, he would be able to see and enjoy the night—alone. There would be a moon, and if the fog did not come, the countryside would be beautiful bathed in moonlight. Kojima had no knowledge of art or poetry. His words, when he spoke, were simple and unlearned. But he possessed a fierce and inarticulate love of beauty—a love which raged within him, longing to free itself in some form of expression. And so Kojima could merely yearn for beauty and, when he encountered it, look at it and worship it in silence. On this clear, moonlit night, he thought, there will be a miracle. The land which is ugly and barren will be touched with silver and transformed into a paradise—and I will see it.

Then he saw the fireman, Tomiji, lumbering toward the locomotive, and he knew that it would soon be time for the train to depart. His hand moved inside of his jacket to where the doll he had bought for his daughter rested.

In the morning, he thought, when she awakens and discovers the doll beside her, her face will glow as though it also had been touched with moonlight. He watched the train, anxious to be aboard it and moving toward his home.

Tomiji had run all the way from Mr. Sato's place, stumbling from the effects of the *awamori*, praying he would not find a wrathful Inouye already there and waiting for him.

He was in luck. Inouye had still not arrived when Tomiji reached the station, and somehow, his head still blurred with drink, his heart pounding from the running, his confused mind barely able to sort out what had happened, he managed to get the fire started and to begin to build up steam in the locomotive's boiler.

This accomplished, Tomiji slumped against the wall of the coal car, his arms leaden, his head cleared by the exertion. He was beginning to remember the afternoon. Had he won or lost at *Mah Jong*? There was some memory of incredible luck and large winnings, but as he searched his pockets he could find no money at all. Was it possible he had lost it all again, or had those devils robbed him—or had he lost the money he had won somewhere along the way? However it had happened, he knew he would have to offer some explanation to his wife when he reached Nemuro. He would get no sleep until he had done that, and he wanted sleep so badly. There would be no rest for him with Inouye insisting on his total vigilance all through the trip. Inouye is a devil too, Tomiji thought bitterly. All the world is filled with devils. The Americans were called devils, and Tomiji did not doubt they were, but they were not the only devils. If the American devils were to come and take me, he thought, and if they would keep me safe from my wife and from Inouye and let me sleep, then I would welcome them. But nothing was going to happen to save him. He was the victim of his wife, of Inouye, and of all the devils in this devil-ridden world— and nothing could save him.

Tomiji watched the roaring fire in the firebox, watched the needle climbing on the pressure gauge, and awaited the arrival of Inouye—his heart filled with tremendous and consuming self-pity.

The evening meal had been finished, and Takeo's grandfather had this time of all times to become talkative. When the old man decided to talk, he invariably inflicted himself on Takeo. It was never a conversation. The boy was not expected to participate other than as an audience.

Takeo was never sure what brought on these spells, but he suspected there was something in a bottle which his mother kept hidden and which, from time to time, his grandfather would discover and drink. Then his mother would take it and hide it in a new place. Takeo had seen his grandfather once, outside the house, furtively drinking from the bottle, and on that occasion he had talked to the boy for a full two hours.

Usually Takeo did not mind having his grandfather in a talkative mood. Sometimes he would actually tell him stories, although they tended to be rambling and, as often as not, he would not finish them satisfactorily because his mind wandered, and he was likely to stray from one story to another without realizing it. But on this evening, Takeo did not want to listen to his grandfather. Takeo's thoughts were too busy with what was to be done during the night. Also, there was no telling how long the old man might go on, and that meant he would be delayed in going to sleep —and that might ruin all of Takeo's plans.

Still there was nothing to do but sit beside his grandfather and listen. They sat on the ground just outside the house. The sun had already gone from the sky, and Takeo could tell it was going to be a clear night. If there is a moon, he thought . . .

"Ah, I remember the time very clearly," his grandfather was saying. "It was when I was a boy of your years, grandson—but I was very different from you, and the world was very different from the world of today."

This was the kind of story Takeo did not like. When his grandfather began a story in this fashion, its point, if there was a point, was invariably to show some fault in Takeo and to expound on the theme that in his grandfather's youth he had been everything which Takeo should be and was not.

But on this evening there was a change.

"I was a bright and intelligent boy—just as you are, grandson. In that way we were much the same. The difference lay in the fact that my father was alive and able to guide me as I grew older. This is not your fault, grandson, but it is your weakness. You live your life with an old man and a woman—and you have need of a father."

Takeo could not recall ever hearing his grandfather speak to him in this way before. There was actually kindness in his voice and in the words he spoke. Takeo listened warily.

"And the world was different also. The world was not as large as it is today. The world then was the house in which I lived with my parents and my brothers and sisters—and the houses of our neighbors whose farms were near ours. There was no other part of the world in those days. And the world was peaceful and beautiful, grandson, and there was plenty of food to fill all our bellies. That is what I remember most of all—that there was plenty of food . . ."

Takeo closed his eyes. He must not permit himself to be lulled by the kindness in his grandfather's voice. He must not be swayed from carrying out his plan. This kindness was only a passing thing. His grandfather had found the hidden bottle and within it he had found not only his tongue but a trace of kindness—but this would wear off, and the bottle would be hidden again—and there would be the endless days of scolding and nagging and the endless nights of snoring—and there must be more to the world than that.

And so to guard himself against the kindness which he wanted so badly from his grandfather, Takeo forced his thoughts to the night which lay ahead—shutting out the grandfather's words, waiting for them to cease so that the old man would go to sleep, and the things which must be done in that night could be done.

By the time Kurita had assembled the other old men who made up his patrol, the full moon was already starting to rise in the darkening sky. Unlike the night before, there was no sign of fog. It looked to be a clear and beautiful evening, a rarity at this time of the year. Kurita considered this a good omen. On such a night it would not be necessary to have the thing the officer had described to him that morning—*radar*. On such a night as this, a man could see what there was to be seen—with his own two eyes and know it for what it truly was—not that Kurita had any reason to believe there would be anything to see, but if there were . . .

As usual, the men grumbled as they prepared to start out. Ordinarily Kurita either joined in their grumbling or ignored them. Tonight, however, he felt constrained to reprimand them.

"Listen to me," he said, in a voice so loud and so strong that he was more surprised than they were. They stopped their muttering, turning their aged, wrinkled faces to look at Kurita with dead eyes. "Listen to me, old men. Last night while we sat doing nothing, only a short distance from where we sat, a great battle was being fought."

The men stirred and looked at one another, shaking their heads and smiling at the sudden madness of Kurita.

"It is true. It was told me by the officer who comes each week to take my report. It was told me because I am the leader here, and it is important that I be kept informed of military matters."

One of the men, a neighbor of Kurita's named Akira, laughed drily. "How could there be a battle near to us and we heard nothing? The officer knows you for a fool, Kurita, and he was playing a fine joke on you."

Kurita gripped his rifle tightly and shook his head with sudden vehemence. "No!" Akira fell back before the violence of his denial. "The officer told me the truth. Out on the sea, there was a great American submarine—a ship that can sink beneath the water and then rise again . . ."

Akira took heart at this. "Listen to him! Now I know he is a fool. There is no such thing as a ship which can sink and then rise again."

Then Osami, a fat, pig-faced farmer, spoke up in a shrill voice. "You are mistaken, Akira. I have heard with my own ears of these submarines. They are fearful ships of war. My brother's own son was serving on one of the Emperor's ships of war, and such a submarine attacked the ship and destroyed it with all its crew, including my nephew. A submarine is indeed a great ship. Tell us of this submarine, Kurita."

Akira was defeated. The other men joined in. "Yes, yes! Tell us of the battle, Kurita!"

Now he had his audience. "The submarine was of the American devils, even as the one of which Osami speaks. It was prowling near the very coast which we patrol each night. One of the brave men who fly in the air for the Emperor saw this submarine with eyes of magic called radar . . ."

Akira rallied for one final effort. "Eyes of magic! There are no eyes which could have seen last night. You know how thick the fog was . . ."

But Kurita stood him down. "With the eyes of this radar he could see! The officer told me. He could see the

American submarine, and when he saw it, his flying machine swooped down like a bird of prey and destroyed the Americans with death dropped from the sky."

The story had its desired effect. The old men were stirred. Their eyes showed glimmers of life. For the first time since Kurita could remember, they seemed anxious to begin their nightly duties.

He rallied them with a final effort. "And we too must be vigilant! If the American devils can come so near to our coast with one of their submarines, then no man among us can allow himself to relax. Tonight—beginning tonight, we must do more than we have done in the past. Our ears must be open for any sound—our eyes must be watchful for anything that moves. Tonight," Kurita pointed his rifle at the rising moon, "we have been given a good sign. The moon will ride in the heavens to give us light that we may see. Though we do not have the magic radar eyes, we have our own, and we must use them . . ." He struggled to think of some way to end his brave speech. "For the Emperor!"

And the old men, even Akira, waved their hands in the air, and from their tired throats echoed his cry.

"For the Emperor!"

The train left Kushiro each evening at exactly ten minutes past the hour of eight. Inouye's insistence on punctuality held for the return trip as rigidly as for the morning run from Nemuro. In the more than two years he had been engineer on this train, he had been late not more than four times, and on each of those occasions the delay had been caused by either a last-minute mechanical breakdown or by military red tape.

It was, therefore, an incident entirely without precedent when Inouye himself reached the Kushiro station fully five minutes past the scheduled time of departure. It was the fault of the accursed woman who was his hostess at the baths. It was her duty to awaken him from the sleep he was privileged to enjoy following his meal. She was a fool, that woman. She was given to making much over Inouye, and ordinarily he was pleased by her attentions, but now she had committed an unpardonable offense. She had told him that he looked so peaceful as he slept that she wanted him to have a few minutes more rest, and he had stormed at her, causing her to weep. He had left her weeping, and this fact filled him with mixed emotions, so that within him, anger and remorse were locked in battle.

His preparations for getting the train under way were hurried and uncertain. He had to meet the slyly malicious eyes of the fireman, Tomiji, who found an unexpected pleasure in Inouye's obvious discomfiture. By the time the steam hissed from the cylinders and the wheels began to turn, the train was a full twenty minutes behind schedule.

Inouye hunched tensely over the controls, his eyes hot and angry, his thoughts bent on one thing only—the absolute necessity to make up that lost time so that his train would reach Nemuro on schedule—at all costs!

When the train reached open country, he could see that it was going to be a clear and fog-free night. The moon was full and bright. The track stretched ahead of him, beckoning him, and he opened the throttle wider, demanding more coal from Tomiji, driving his train through the night toward its destination—straining with his whole self to regain his mastery of the thing which was his whole reason for being—cursing the creature of steel and steam, even as he loved it above all other things.

At twenty hundred hours the *Mudskipper* surfaced within half a mile of the position from which the landing party would be launched. The rubber boat was brought topside immediately to be inflated under Jake Stock's supervision. Tolliver remained on the bridge with Wes Clayton until the submarine had reached the launch position. Like the others in the landing party Tolliver was dressed entirely in black, and his face had been smeared with lampblack. This final touch had been decided on when it became obvious that it would be a bright and clear night.

The sea was calm, and as the *Mudskipper* cut through the water, her bow marked a line of brilliant phosphorescence. The outline of the coast was clearly visible ahead.

"Hell, Captain," Clayton muttered. "It's like having a damned spotlight on you. Makes you feel kind of naked, doesn't it?"

Tolliver was fascinated by the moon. He had never seen it so huge, he thought. There was something about it which drew and held him. "It's a good omen, Wes," he said. "The whole thing will go much faster and easier on a night like this."

"Yeah, I guess so." Clayton did not sound convinced. "You're all set on the pickup plan?"

"Yes, sir." Clayton repeated his instructions. "I'll have the boat at the pickup position by twenty-three forty. I'll run with decks awash to show as little silhouette as possible until we actually sight you. We probably won't need a signal because of the moonlight, but we'll use the three shorts and three longs just in case."

Tolliver nodded. "Right. If everything goes on schedule, the people over there are going to be too busy wondering what happened to worry about anything out here. The train should blow shortly after we've shoved off from the beach." He laughed softly, feeling the undercurrent of excitement beginning to stir him. "It would be something to see up close, wouldn't it, Wes, but I guess we should be able to get some of the effect from where we'll be."

Clayton cleared his throat uneasily. "Look, Captain, one last time—let me go instead of you."

"Afraid not, Wes." He said it absently, his eyes and attention caught and held now by the sharply defined line of the Hokkaido coast. He had, in effect, already relinquished control of the *Mudskipper* to Clayton. He was free of the submarine and he yearned toward the land, in his mind creating pictures of what would be seen there— the barren countryside, the railway track, the train itself . . .

Clayton was still talking, still going over the routine plans which had been set for him. "And if, for any damned reason at all, Captain, you can't make the rendezvous while it's still dark. I mean, if for *any* reason you can't make it, then I'll have the boat right back here as soon as it's dark tomorrow . . ."

"All right, Wes!" Clayton's voice was starting to annoy him. The man talked too much. He had been handed a simple bit of responsibility, and he was already in a state of panic. It's a good thing the war is almost over, Tolliver thought. If it went on much longer they'd be using men like Wes Clayton for command posts. He found himself depressed by his thoughts. The war was almost over, wasn't it? It was not just a rumor. How long? Would it be

a week or a month or a year? It could come at any time
—and he toyed with a new fantasy, a fascinating one.

Suppose, just suppose it came with the next day. Suppose that somewhere, even at this very moment, the Japanese were deciding, had already decided, that it was
senseless and useless to continue the war. Suppose a paper
was being written or a message was being coded for trans-
mission, asking for an end to the fighting.

It could happen that way, and when it happened, the
word would be flashed out to all of the forces in the Pa-
cific. There would be an immediate cessation of hostili-
ties. That moment would come one day, that moment
which hung in the hairline balance between war and
peace, when on one side of a heartbeat a man could kill
his enemy, and, on the other side, the enemy had admitted defeat and was thereby immune to killing. He thought
about a torpedo which had just been fired at an enemy
ship, or a bomb which had just been released from a plane
and was plummeting toward an enemy city, or a bullet
which had just been fired from a rifle and was crashing
through the air toward the body of an enemy soldier.
What was the meaning of peace to these instruments of
death? They could not be called back, could not be
stopped. They were blind, save for the eyes which had set
them into motion, and, once started, they could only continue to their destination of destruction.

The landing party, he thought, was possessed of that
same marvelous inevitability. Once we are free of the
Mudskipper, once we have been set on our course, no
word can call us back.

Only let us have that much time!

He was praying, he realized, and was surprised. He had
not prayed in so many years, and he did not even know to

whom or to what he prayed.

"Okay, Captain. This is about it." Wes Clayton leaned over the hatch and called, "All stopped!"

Tolliver's hand dropped to the automatic in the holster at his waist. It felt very good. He called down to the men on the forward deck. "All set down there, Jake?"

Stock's eyes, as he looked up toward the bridge, caught the moonlight for an instant. "Yes, sir."

"All right, Wes." Tolliver turned to the Executive Officer. "We'll see you soon. How does it feel to have a command of your own?"

Clayton's laugh was unsteady. "I'll let you know, Captain. Take it easy now, for Pete's sake. Good luck, Captain!"

"Thank you, Wes." There was genuine affection in Clayton's voice, he thought. What a fool the man was!

Without further conversation, Tolliver swung himself down the ladder to the deck. Moving forward, he reached the group of men standing beside the rubber boat. Weslowski and Lyle were holding the bulky object which was the bomb. John Barringer had the electrical materials needed for wiring the bomb in a waterproof case which had been strapped on his back like a knapsack.

Its engines stopped, the *Mudskipper* had lost steerage and was wallowing slightly in the calm sea.

"All right," Tolliver said tersely, "let's go!"

Schroeder and Tatum pushed the rubber boat over the side, holding on to ropes which pulled the boat in until it was rubbing against the hull of the submarine. Quickly Jake Stock dropped into the boat, and Tolliver followed him. Then the two men holding the bomb knelt and placed it in a sling which had been improvised for that purpose. Gingerly they lowered it toward the two officers in the boat

"Got it, Jake?" Tolliver was surprised at the weight of the bomb. He and Jake Stock received it and lowered it to the bottom of the boat. They were not yet taking any water over the side, thanks to the calmness of the sea.

"Okay, Captain." Stock motioned to the men still on the deck of the submarine. "Come on, you guys!"

Two of the sailors who were not members of the landing party took over the lines holding the boat while Schroeder and Tatum dropped down into it. The last man to leave the submarine was Barringer.

"Cast off!" Tolliver called, and the men on the deck tossed the lines down to them. "All right, let's go!"

Lyle, Tatum, Schroeder and Weslowski had the paddles. The boat was pushed off from the submarine's hull, and as the paddles dipped into the water, it began its painfully slow movement away from the *Mudskipper* and toward the distant shore.

Tolliver was seated in the stern, and Jake Stock crouched in the bow. In the very center of the boat was the bomb. Tolliver turned to look back at the *Mudskipper* only once. It was sharply silhouetted against the moonlit sky. He could see Wes Clayton on the bridge, one hand raised and waving at them. Then he turned away and set his gaze on the shore.

They were under way! The torpedo was launched—the bomb released—the bullet fired! No power could turn them back now! The fish which sought its prey on land would not be denied.

Sixteen

⚓

Tomiji had come to the point of actually hating the engineer, Inouye. Once he had dared admit this fact to himself, it gave him great pleasure. Indeed, he thought, he had undoubtedly hated Inouye all along, but until this night, until Inouye had demonstrated his human weakness by arriving late for the departure of the train from Kushiro, Tomiji had been afraid to recognize the true nature of his feelings. Now Inouye had revealed himself to be a mere mortal, with the failings and vulnerabilities of mortals. He had driven Tomiji before, but always before it had been the driving of a miserable man by an infallible superman. Now, as Inouye called for more coal, he was abusing Tomiji in order to cover up his own inadequacy. And, as Tomiji sweated and shoveled coal into the firebox —his head throbbing and his heart pounding with the effort—he seized upon his newfound hatred of Inouye, finding in it a focal point toward which he could direct all of the misery which filled his life. And that hatred gave him new strength, so that the shovel became a feather in his hands. He fed the raging fire with a fury which consumed him as the flames consumed the coal.

And, for the first time, Tomiji, like Inouye, became a part of the locomotive, his body and his hate-filled mind fusing with the steel monster as it hurtled through the night.

The soldier Kojima sat cross legged in the empty freight car. His rifle lay on the floor beside him. He had left the door to the car open, and he watched the countryside rushing past him—a blurred vision of moon-drenched splendor. The train, he knew, was traveling at a greater rate of speed than usual. The car swayed and lurched constantly, and the harsh song of the wheels on the track possessed an urgency Kojima had never before heard. But eventually the movement of the train became something he no longer noticed, and the sound of the wheels faded into the background, while Kojima surrendered himself to beauty and contentment. His lips moved in the words of an old song, a song which his mother had sung to him and which he had almost forgotten:

When the moon is full and bright
Fear is driven from the night.

Rush on, Train, Kojima thought. At the end of this night's journey awaits love and peace.

His hands went once again to the little doll he carried close to his body, and a great sense of joy flooded over him. Taking the doll from its resting place, he cradled it in his arms and rocked it with the rocking, swaying motion of the train, and a shaft of moonlight penetrated the

freight car and fell across the painted face, and he sang
the song once again.

When the moon is full and bright
Fear is driven from the night.

The moonlight penetrated the window of Takeo's
house. He lay stretched out on his bed and waited for the
sign that his mother slept. His grandfather had finally
given up and gone off to bed, and his snoring was already
steady, indicating that he was asleep for the duration of
the night. However, Takeo's mother had been restless.
Once, Takeo thought he heard her weeping—softly, almost soundlessly—but he could not be certain. He could
not remember ever having seen his mother weep, and the
thought disturbed him. Was it possible, he wondered, that
she knew what he was planning to do? Was it possible
that she knew he was going away from her that night, and
did she care enough to weep for this? Once he was
tempted to creep out of his bed and go to her to see if
there might be some way he could comfort her. But if he
did that, then she might know something was wrong.
Sleep might be even longer in coming to her, and the
thing which must be done that night could not be done.
So Takeo waited, fighting to hold off the sleepiness which
threatened him. He forced himself to think about the
train, and the place on the tracks where he had found the
sign and made his own answering sign. It was to this place
he must go. The moonlight would make it easy to find.
This was a good sign, a sign that he had not been mistaken in choosing this night. The good demon who had
made the cross for him to see had arranged that the night
should be clear and that the moon should be full and
bright to aid Takeo.

Then he heard his mother's snores gently join those of his grandfather, and they sounded sad in a strange way, as though her weeping continued, even in her sleep.

Very quietly Takeo rose from his bed and slipped into his clothing. He had hidden the knife under his mattress, and now he retrieved it and placed it in the rope which held up his trousers. Now he was ready, but before he left he walked softly over to where his mother lay sleeping. The moonlight partially revealed her face. He had never seen his mother when she was asleep, and he stood gazing at her with wonder. He would not have believed she could look so young. All of the lines which marked her face when she was awake had vanished, and she looked like a girl, a beautiful girl. But he had been right about her weeping. There were still tear stains on her cheeks. For a long time Takeo stood beside her and watched her face. If she were to awake, if her eyes were to open and see him standing there, then she would not let him go. She would keep him with her always. He was tempted to lean over her, and to touch her face ever so gently as a way of saying goodbye. His hand went toward her, but it stopped just before the fingers reached her face.

And Takeo knew that tears were also filling his eyes and running down his cheeks, and that he must go—quickly, before he gave way to the weakness which was growing within him. He drew back his hand, wiping the tears from his face defiantly, and made his way to the door. Once it was open, once he had stepped outside of his house into the night which was filled with the magic light of the moon, then Takeo did not look back at his house again.

"On this night," Kurita told his men, "instead of remaining always together, we will patrol more efficiently, in a more military fashion."

He had divided the group into three small sections and assigned each section one portion of the coastal area to patrol. He took charge of one section which included his critic, Akira. It was agreed that the men would search diligently all the territory between the shore and the railroad tracks, taking only brief periods of rest.

"Leave no stone unturned," Kurita had exhorted them. "Remember that the Emperor depends on us just as he depends on every soldier. If the American submarine could come so close to our shore last night, then anything could happen. The war has moved nearer and nearer to us, and one night—perhaps a night like this—perhaps this very night, the war might actually move upon this very shore, and if that should happen, then we are the soldiers who would be called upon to defend our soil."

It was a very stirring speech, and the old men reacted well to it, raising their voices in shouts of defiance against the enemy and vowing to fight like demons should any enemy dare show himself. The bright light shed by the moon added to their courage. They were filled suddenly with the old, half-remembered vigor of their youth, and Kurita felt a great sense of pride in them and in himself as their leader.

Now, he thought to himself, let the American devils come. We will be ready for them. And the boast turned into a prayer, for in his heart Kurita knew that there was indeed a magic to this night, that the courage and strength he had found and had been able to impart to the other old men would not last. It belonged to this night, and on future nights the moon would be gone, and the courage would be gone, and they would become weary old men again, filled with the fears and the doubts and the weaknesses of old men in a world of darkness.

And so he prayed to the gods.

Yes, let them come, let them come tonight!

No matter how he drove his fireman, himself, or the locomotive, there seemed to be no way he could make up the lost time. Inouye felt desperation building within him. He hated the moonlight, because it revealed the world to him at a time when he would have preferred to have the world hidden from him, and himself from the world. He felt naked and exposed, all his weaknesses placed on display for hostile eyes to look upon and laugh at.

The dreams which sustained him were being threatened. The image of himself as the master of a mighty ship was blurred and fading, and in its place he was beginning to see another image—the image of a middle-aged, middle-class man, without distinction. He saw a man who was not fit to fight and instead went through the glorious time of war operating a wretched train between two wretched towns, masking the abject disgrace of this service by creating a fantasy world in which absolute efficiency was the key. *To run the train on time!* It came down to that, and somehow he must regain that vital element of the fantasy.

"More steam!" he screamed at the fireman. "Give me more steam!"

And his gloved hand pushed the throttle forward as Inouye leaned out of the cab, his eyes searching ahead as the train sped through the night toward its destination.

Jake Stock was almost certain that they had managed to reach the shore at virtually the same place he and Freddie Baldwin had landed the night before. The little alcove was there all right. He motioned with one hand, pointing toward the opening in the rocks.

"We can leave the boat in there."

Getting the bomb up the sheer rise was not simple. The problem was finally solved by using the sling which had been made for loading it from the *Mudskipper*'s deck to the rubber boat. When this task had been completed, Stock paused to take in the scene around them. It looked quite different than it had on the previous night. Then the fog had prevented their seeing anything. Now the entire desolate landscape was revealed in the bright moonlight.

Jonathan Tolliver stood beside him. His voice was hushed and oddly strained. "It's like another world."

"Yes, sir." Stock glanced at Tolliver. The *Mudskipper*'s Commanding Officer stood erect, gazing out to sea. For the moment he seemed oblivious of where he was or of the other men around him. One of the men, Stock could not tell which, cleared his throat. "Captain," Stock murmured finally, "we'd better get started . . ."

Tolliver nodded slowly, his eyes still fixed on the bright streak of moonlight which stretched across the water. "Yes." Then he stirred, slapped his hands together soundlessly and showed his teeth in a strange smile. "Let's go, Jake. Station the lookouts, and you lead the way. You've been here before."

Stock fought back the temptation to ask why Tolliver had come at all. He knew the answer, and it was better left alone.

He stationed Fritz Schroeder and Finley Tatum at the edge of the drop above the place where the rubber boat was secured. "Now get this straight," he told them. "If you spot anyone, or anything, don't panic. Your first responsibility is to be undetected, so keep down as much as possible, and don't go shooting except in a real emergency. You know approximately when to expect us back, and you won't have any trouble spotting us." Stock glanced over to where Tolliver was standing. He was paying no attention to Stock and the two men. "Remember one thing," Stock muttered, "if anything happens to us, you're on your own. Give it every chance, but if it comes to the worse, get the hell away from here and back to the boat. Schroeder, you're in charge, and it's your decision. Understood?"

Fritz Schroeder shifted the submachine gun uneasily from one hand to the other. "Yes, sir."

Stock nodded. "Okay. Stay loose, and we'll be back as soon as we can."

Finley Tatum whispered loudly, "Good luck, Mr. Stock."

"Yeah," Stock muttered. Then he moved over to Tolliver. "All set, Captain."

The five men who were to move on to the railway tracks gathered around Tolliver. He glanced around at them, his eyes bright with excitement and gleaming against the blackened skin of his face. He seemed to be forcing his attention to the task at hand. "From here on," he said finally, "no more talking than absolutely necessary. Jake, you take the lead. Barringer next, and be sure you warn the men carrying the bomb of anything they might stumble over. I'll bring up the rear." He laughed softly. "That's to make sure nobody changes his mind and starts back." He said this as a joke, but his eyes touched Jake Stock, and Stock knew it was really a warning to him.

Despite the brightness of the night, they moved slowly. The two men carrying the bomb set the pace. Just as they reached the stretch of high grass, Stock stopped suddenly and threw up one hand.

Behind him, Barringer whispered, "What is it?"

He had heard something. Stock could not be sure what he had heard. It had no definition or form. It was more an awareness of sound than anything else. He motioned Barringer to be quiet. A moment later Jonathan Tolliver had moved up to stand beside him.

"What are you trying to start?" he hissed.

"Wait!"

The men stood, rooted in their tracks, straining to hear. Then the sound became clearer. There were voices, but it was impossible to tell what they were saying.

"Get down!" Stock dropped to his knees. The other men, with the exception of Tolliver, followed suit, and Stock reached up one hand and pulled Tolliver down.

Now the voices grew louder, and Stock cautiously raised his head above the high grass to look around. He saw them then—three men moving on a path which would take them directly in front of the place where the men from the *Mudskipper* were crouched. They were perhaps fifty yards away and moving very slowly.

Stock was aware that a hand was gripping his arm. He glanced around at Tolliver, whose eyes were glints of light. The fingers dug into Stock's arm.

They could see the men more clearly now. They were not soldiers—more like farmers, Stock thought, or fishermen. He could not make out their faces, but they moved like old men—probably on their way home from the fields. One of them carried what looked like a kind of pitchfork across his shoulder.

"A gun!" Tolliver's voice muttered in his ear. "One of them has a gun!"

Stock could see it now. One of the men, the one in the lead, did carry a rifle in one hand. When they reached a point almost directly in front of the Americans' position, the three men stopped, and the man with the gun seemed to be scolding the other two. His voice was raised to a shrill pitch, and he was pointing and gesticulating vigorously. The other two men hung back, shaking their heads. From what Stock could tell, the one man wanted them to keep on moving, while the other two wanted to stop. At last the man with the gun evidently won his point, and the men walked on—the two of them with obvious reluctance, grumbling as they went. Stock waited until they were out of sight. Then he drew a deep breath.

"Okay," he whispered. "Let's go."

Only then did Tolliver's grip on his arm relax. And when he looked at Tolliver, Stock felt a stab of panic. The man's eyes were wide and staring. He did not speak, falling back to take his place at the rear of the group, but Stock knew he had been looking at the face of a man who, for that moment, was on the verge of collapse—or worse.

Seventeen

⚓

KURITA WAS VERY angry. The enthusiasm he had managed
to stir in the old men of his patrol at the beginning of the
night was already dissipated, and all they wanted to do
was to find some comfortable place to sit and doze and
gossip among themselves and wait for the night to pass.
But Kurita remained adamant. The two men, Akira and
Osami, who were with him, were the worst grumblers of
the lot. It was only by making dire threats, by actually
pretending that there might be something amiss, that he
had been able to drive them to continue to maintain their
vigilance along with him.

"There is nothing to be found," Osami had whined.
Osami was so fat that he tired very easily. "You drive us
without cause, Kurita. We are old, and our bodies need to
rest. Why must we stay on our feet and walk—always
walk?"

And Kurita had lied. "Because," he said, "I have reason
to believe that on this very night there is great danger. I

feel it here." He touched his chest with one clenched fist. "It is our duty to be alert, to search as though the enemy were already here in great numbers."

"There is no enemy here," Akira muttered. "There will never be an enemy here."

And Kurita had lifted his head and looked carefully all around, while Akira and Osami watched him. "There is *something*," he told them. "Like the magic radar, I can sense that there is *something* . . ."

And, at that moment, he was shocked to realize that he was not simply making up a story to convince the other men. He did have the *feeling*—like the one he had had the night before—that there was *something* out there in the night. He and the other two men stood at the edge of an area which was thick with high rough sea grass. As far as Kurita's eyes could see in the bright moonlight there was nothing. Yet the feeling persisted, more strongly than before. The hair lifted on the back of Kurita's neck, and for the first time since he had started out that night, he was forced to consider the actual possibility that he and his men might encounter *something*—not an imaginary or fantasy *something*, but a *something* of substance—a flesh and blood *something*. His brave words and his boasts and his exhortations to his men had been based, he knew, on a *something* of the mind. Now, standing exposed in the moonlight, his eyes searched for that which he feared to find.

Akira and Osami watched him. He must not reveal to them his weakness and his fear. He, who had for this one night, assumed a position of true importance, must not lose face—not yet. Whatever it was that he sensed—that he felt with his whole being now—whatever it was might simply go away. He might never be called upon to face it and deal with it.

"Come on," he called to his two companions, struggling to keep the fear from showing in his voice. "Come on, you lazy old men. We must continue our search. Remember the Emperor depends on us. The man who does not do his duty will have to answer to me—to Kurita!"

And, still grumbling, they followed him as he continued his search through the night, for the terrible thing he prayed he would not find.

The men from the *Mudskipper* reached the railway tracks at twenty-two thirty. The scene was exactly as Tolliver had pictured it in his mind so many times since the first sighting of the train. Even the moonlight which gently bathed the barren countryside was consistent with the way he had thought of the scene. He was exhilarated by this, and the weariness and tension diminished with the sense of vindication which came with actually being there.

"It is beautiful," he murmured finally. "Beautiful!"

He had come up to stand beside Jake Stock, who shot a glance at him and then looked away. Tolliver caught that look. Suddenly he realized that Stock was watching him —watching for what? Suppose, he thought, suppose Jake Stock, even now, had ideas about stopping the plan to destroy the train. He had always been confident that he could control Stock, absolutely. Now, for the first time, he had doubts. Stock seemed stronger than before. Tolliver glanced around at the others. What were they thinking? If Stock were to try something, how would they react?

He could feel panic rising within him, and he was having difficulty focusing his thoughts.

"All right, Jake . . ." He could hear his own voice as

though it belonged to another man. It sounded all right. It was steady, confident. "Go ahead. Get started on it." He glanced at his watch, easily reading the dial in the moonlight. "We ought to be clear of here by twenty-three hundred." Then he gazed at the tracks, following them with his eyes as far as he could see. It was so beautiful. Like sweet, forgotten music out of the past, words came back to him . . .

"The road was a ribbon of moonlight . . ." he murmured.

"What's that, Captain?" Jake Stock had turned to look at him again.

Tolliver started. "It's nothing, Jake. A poem—about a highwayman."

Stock stared for a moment, then nodded. "Yes, sir."

Tolliver watched as the big man squatted down with Barringer and the other two men at the track. They were beginning to wire the bomb to the two microswitches. Tolliver was apart from them, and he watched until, without knowing why or how, his attention passed beyond the men, beyond the thing they were doing.

It is the moonlight, he told himself, that enables me to see so plainly the thing which will happen. I have watched it so many times . . .

The train rushing through the night, huge and powerful and beautiful in the moonlight . . .

My eyes! They are so heavy. Hardly keep them open . . .

The place where death awaits the train is here. Here! And the train rushes toward it, coming nearer and nearer —the split second which hangs between life and death— between beauty and ruin—this was the instant which rested completely in his control.

I see the torpedo against the side of a ship. The water flung toward the sky. My torpedo!

And the vision he had of the scene, the train actually stopped in that split second, hanging as it were in space, held back by his will to be considered and desired and loved and marked for destruction . . .

Let me sleep! Give me the rest I must have!

And then, by his will, he released the train and sent it into the awful fiery grip of death. And he watched as the train was battered with the dreadful fist of his instrument of destruction—ripped into bits, shredded in flame and smoke . . .

Not yet! I must not stop yet! It is still a dream, but the dream is almost reality. Then I can rest.

A part of him was aware of the sweat which poured from his body now, coursing down his face, chilling him until he shivered in the night air. A part of him stood to one side and watched over him, guarding him from the blackness which threatened to engulf him.

He would hold out long enough. There had been a moment when he had almost slipped, and he knew Jake Stock had seen this, but Stock was busy now. By the time Stock could turn his attention back to Tolliver, it would be too late. Nothing could stop it now!

And the minutes crawled by as the men worked over the bomb, fixing the instrument of his desire, and Tolliver stood and watched over them, holding himself together desperately—against the time, the time, the time . . .

Takeo had walked very slowly from his house toward the tracks. He knew it would be some time yet before the train came, and also he was reluctant to go swiftly. It was as if he could retain something of the life he was leaving for a little longer if he walked slowly. He did not look back. It would have been a mistake to look back, for if he had, he might have weakened and returned to his mother. It was not until his house was completely out of sight that he was able to fix his attention completely on what lay ahead. Then, and only then, his step quickened. Excitement built within him, and suddenly he felt very light, as though some awful weight had been lifted from him. He wanted to run and laugh aloud, but it would not be seemly to do that. He was entering upon the life of a man, and men did not run and laugh aloud. Still, he did walk more quickly, and he could feel the smile on his lips . . .

Remembering the sign he had found on the railway tracks that morning, he wondered if the good demon who had placed it there had come again and seen his answering mark. Suddenly it occurred to Takeo that the demon might actually be there now. He stopped, frightened by that possibility. True, he had decided it was a *good* demon, but demons, good or bad, were not to be taken lightly. Still, he reasoned, he was beginning the life of a man, and a man must be able to deal with the things a boy might run away from. He resumed his steps, more slowly now, building his courage for whatever he might find.

He headed directly for the spot where the marks had been made. There was plenty of time before the train arrived, but he wanted to be there . . .

Then he saw them!

Instinctively he dropped to the ground, his fingers clawing at the earth, his face turned downward, his body shaking violently. Then, summoning all his courage, he slowly raised his head until he could see. There were many of them! He had thought in terms of a single demon, a demon whose physical form Takeo could not even imagine, but surely something unearthly in appearance. But these demons seemed to have the forms of men, and there were—he counted carefully—five of them! Still trembling, fighting the impulse to run away as fast as his legs would carry him, Takeo edged nearer, crawling along to keep out of view, not knowing whether the demons had the magic power to know he was there even if they could not see him.

Three of the demons were kneeling beside the tracks. He was certain they were at the place where the marks had been made. Was it possible they were examining his mark, wondering what it meant, or, being demons, would they not know what it meant? If so, they would be expecting him. Another demon stood over those three, while the fifth stood apart, watching the others.

Takeo crawled still closer. Suddenly the demon who stood apart from the others turned so that his face was caught in the moonlight. Takeo gasped. The face was black! The suspicion that these might not be demons, but men, was now gone. No men had faces which were black. He could see the eyes, strange and bright and glittering. The demon was tall, taller than any man could be.

He knew he should go to them and let them know he had come as he had promised, but something held him back. He could see now that the demons were busy with some object they had placed beside the tracks. It was large and black, and it looked evil, just as the face of that tall demon had looked evil. Takeo could not believe that a good demon could have a face which was black, and suddenly the truth came to him. These were not good demons. If indeed it had been a good demon who had placed the white mark for Takeo to find, then these must be his enemies. Perhaps they had found the good demon and destroyed him or made him their prisoner. There were so many of them that despite the fact they were evil, they might have been able to overpower a single good demon. Now they were preparing something, and Takeo knew instinctively that it represented a danger to the train—to *his* train! That black, ominous-looking object was something created by the evil demons to harm the train. He could even hear sounds now, as though the demons were talking among themselves, but the words sounded strange—further proof that these indeed were not humans. No human would make sounds.

Takeo clung to the earth, his heart pounding, all of his plans and dreams now suddenly threatened. His instinct was to get away, to flee from these black, evil creatures back to the safety of his home, back to his mother and grandfather and his life as a boy. But, if he did that, then he knew his train was doomed. His dreams were doomed. He must stay here. He must watch these demons, and, if the opportunity presented itself, he must somehow try to save the train.

Jake Stock swore softly. "Come on, you guys, what's the holdup?"

John Barringer shook his head. "It's this second microswitch, Mr. Stock. I can't get this doggoned thing to hold steady. It keeps sliding off at an angle."

Stock glanced at his watch. It was twenty-three ten. "Okay, okay," he muttered. "Just hurry it up!"

He looked over to where Tolliver was standing. The Commanding Officer of the *Mudskipper* was not even watching the work on the bomb. Instead he was gazing in the direction from which the train would come, a strange smile playing on his lips, and he was rubbing his hands together in a kind of washing motion, over and over again. Without knowing why, Stock shuddered.

"There!" Barringer straightened. "I think that ought to hold it. Now let me double check the connections, and we'll be done."

"Good! Now, let's get the hell out of here!" Stock hesitated and turned to look once again at Tolliver. Then he glanced back at the other three men, all of whom were likewise looking at their Commanding Officer. Tolliver was still engrossed in his own thoughts, and he appeared completely unaware of the presence of the others. Finally Jake Stock moved to him. "Captain . . ."

There was no answer. Stock repeated, a little louder, "Captain, we're ready to shove off."

Slowly, as though he were tearing himself reluctantly away from some totally absorbing thing, Tolliver turned to look at Stock. His gaze, Stock thought, went quite past or through him. "What?" Then, with an obvious effort, the eyes focused on Stock. The man's concentration, Stock realized, was achieved only with the greatest difficulty. "Yes, Jake, I heard you. Are you ready for me to check the bomb?"

"Captain," Stock said quickly, "I've checked it out. We're running short on time. That train is going to be coming along here any minute now."

Tolliver shook his head and smiled. "Oh, no, Jake. Not that easy. I know what you want, but it's no use. You'd like to save it, wouldn't you?" His voice hardened, rising in pitch. "We don't leave here until I've checked every detail of that bomb! You thought you could get it done while I was busy with something else and then leave it here with a faulty connection and then it wouldn't go off, and you could pretend it was an accident! I know what you wanted to do, Jake, and that's why I insisted on coming!"

He stopped, his face contorted in fury, struggling to bring himself under control. The three enlisted men were staring at him in disbelief. Stock's mind was a turmoil. There were only two possible courses of action. Either he could make the decision here and now that Tolliver was temporarily ill and take charge of the operation, or he could pamper the man long enough to get him back to the *Mudskipper*, where Wes Clayton could worry about what to do.

"I'm sorry, Captain," he said. "Of course you should check it. It's okay though. I swear."

Tolliver nodded. "That's better." He seemed almost normal again. "I'm sorry, Jake. I didn't mean to blow off that way. It's just that this—means quite a lot to me."

"Yes, sir. Now, we'd better check it out right away, Captain. We don't want to take a chance . . ."

"That's right, Jake." Tolliver smiled and slapped his hands together. "All right, then." He walked over, past the three enlisted men, and knelt beside the bomb. "It looks very good." His hands touched the leads from the microswitches gently. "Very neat, gentlemen. This should be close enough to do the job, I think." He glanced over his shoulder at them with a pleased smile. "Congratulations are in order. I want each of you to know that I am going to recommend you for decorations."

Stock caught a quick glance from John Barringer. The Electrician's Mate raised his eyebrows in an unspoken question. Stock shook his head.

"Yes. Very good. Very good indeed." Tolliver placed his hands lovingly on the bomb. "Mischief, thou art afoot," he murmured. "Take thou what course thou wilt."

Then he got to his feet. "All right, Jake. We can go now."

Stock motioned urgently with his hand. "Yes, sir. Come on, you guys, let's *move out!*"

And at that precise moment the first shot rang out . . .

Kurita was afraid to continue his patrol alone, but when Akira and Osami finally refused to go on without an hour's rest, he had forced himself to make one more inspection of the area. This time he had chosen to follow the very edge of the rocks which jutted out over the sea. The moon was directly overhead now, and the sea and land were bathed in a light which was almost as bright as the day. It was pure luck that Kurita saw the two men before they saw him. Their backs were to him, and he was able to scramble behind a rock before they turned back in his direction. He was no farther from them than the distance a boy might be able to throw a stone. His heart pounding, his hands slippery with sweat as they grasped at the rifle, Kurita peered from behind the rock at the men. They looked huge, silhouetted against the sky. And they carried weapons! He could see their faces, and they were black, but Kurita knew them to be Americans.

Why were they here? Surely they were not alone, but where were the others—and how many were there? Kurita's mind was feverish with indecision. What should he do now? If he went back to find his companions, the Americans might escape. And yet there were two—at least two of them—and he was alone, an old man, he thought with a great surge of self-pity. It was not right that he alone should be expected to engage a whole army of Americans.

But the glory! He must not forget the glory. Perhaps

these two were all the Americans that were here. And Kurita had the advantage of surprise. If he could capture these two and lead them back to where the other old men took their ease, his reputation would be made forever. Through all the countryside, the name of Kurita would be heard and praised. The officer would be very surprised and very proud of him—to have captured two Americans all alone . . .

His trembling finger curled around the trigger of the rifle. He hoped he would not have to shoot. He did not want to shoot. The very thought of the sound of the rifle frightened him. He wondered if he had to shoot, would he remember how to work the bolt of the rifle. Perhaps it was all a mistake. Perhaps he should simply steal away and pretend to himself he had seen nothing. Perhaps . . .

"Stand!"

He was on his feet and moving toward the two men, pointing his rifle at them, calling to them. "Stand, or I shoot!"

The men whirled toward him, and he heard their voices shouting words he could not understand, and he realized too late that they could not understand him, could not know he was offering them a chance to surrender. His eyes glazed with fear as he saw them raise their weapons toward him, and his finger jerked convulsively on the trigger of the rifle. He saw one of the men spin about and start to fall, then actually saw the flame spurt from the weapon of the other man and heard the beginning of the staccato burst at the same instant his own life was smashed into a blackness which exploded in a seething mass of red through which he could see—almost see—something which he recognized but could not name—and then there was nothing . . .

The single shot was followed instantly by a burst of machine gun fire. Stock had his forty-five out and was yelling, "Let's go! Keep low, but *move!*"

The others needed no urging, moving past him on the run toward the place where they had left the boat. There was only silence following that one savage exchange of shots, but Stock was in no mood to speculate about what might have happened. The thing to do now was to get the hell out!

"Captain!"

He had gone some fifty yards when he realized Tolliver was not with them. Whirling, he saw Tolliver had stopped and was standing, looking back at the railway tracks, head lifted as though he were listening for something.

"Captain! Come on!" Stock ran back to him and seized his arm, but Tolliver shook him off.

"Listen, Jake!" His voice had a hint of sadness in it. "Listen! It's coming—the train is coming!"

At first Stock could hear nothing, but then he did catch a kind of sound—almost an impression of a sound.

"Captain, we've got to get back and find out what's—"

"There it is!" Tolliver pointed excitedly, and then Stock saw it too—the single beam of light and then, dimly, the silhouette of the train itself with smoke tracing a black, curving line against the sky.

"Just for a minute, Jake." Tolliver's voice had the pleading quality of a child's. "I want to watch it just for a minute . . ."

Takeo heard the shots, saw the figures who were at the tracks look up, startled, then begin to run. Then he understood that the evil was being done not by demons, but by men—and this understanding was the true beginning of his manhood. He did not know who the men were, but he knew them for men, because they had been frightened by the shots. Then it came to him who they were. They were worse than evil demons, worse than devils. They were the men who had killed his father—the Americans, and now in some way they were trying to harm Takeo's train.

Whatever the thing was that they had been putting on the tracks was intended to hurt the train, and he was the only one who knew. He was the only one who could save the train! The men had run away, and Takeo heard the sound of the train. Scrambling to his feet he started to run toward the tracks. Whatever the thing was—if he could get it away—if he could warn the train!

By the time he reached the tracks he was out of breath, and he knew he was crying, but it was not a child's crying. It was the crying of a man's anger, of a man's love and hatred. He saw the thing. It looked too big for him to move, but he bent over it, straining to lift it. It was no use! There were things that looked like wires running from the heavy black object to the tracks themselves. Takeo's knowledge of electricity was rudimentary, but he did know that power could pass through wire—power which could accomplish mighty things. The power must run through these wires to do—what? Was this the thing which controlled the power to harm the train?

It was his only chance. Desperately, sobbing with fear and rage, his fingers tugged at the wires, trying to pull them free.

And the tracks vibrated with ever-increasing force as the train thundered nearer . . .

Tolliver saw the small figure running toward the spot where they had placed the bomb. For a moment he saw it as himself, as the boy he had been on that afternoon in the basement of his home, running toward the tracks of the toy train with which his older brother was playing, and he smiled triumphantly at the clarity of the memory. There he was, about to accomplish once again that marvelous act of love and destruction. He had seen it many times before, but never so clearly. He could ignore the insistent voice of Stock, who was trying to pull him away. He must not leave! This was too wonderful a sight to miss—to be able to watch himself destroy his brother's train all over again—to stand like this, a witness . . .

But something was wrong! The boy was not going to destroy the train! He was not going to pound it into pieces with his fists! That boy was not Jonathan Tolliver! He was trying to save the train—pulling at the wires to disconnect them!

"No!"

The scream that tore from his throat battered down the barrier, opening the floodgates of his madness. He felt it rushing upon him, knew one searing instant of panic, and then welcomed it as it engulfed him.

And he was running—running with the speed of the wind, filled with the exultation of his love for the thing which must be destroyed.

Takeo had succeeded in getting one of the wires free when the man reached him. The boy saw the blackened face, twisted into a hideous mask, and he knew that a man could be as frightening as a demon. The man was screaming words which Takeo could not understand, and he seized the boy, trying to get his hands at his throat. Takeo reached for his father's knife as the hands gripped his windpipe. His breath was being choked off, and the blackened face blurred.

The knife was his! Desperately he slashed with it, felt it rip into the flesh of the man's arm, heard the high scream of pain. Then the hands released his throat, and the man flung him aside, sending him sprawling and gasping for breath. *The knife!* He had lost the knife! The man, blood already running down from the wound in his arm, bent over the thing at the tracks, trying to replace the wire Takeo had pulled free—working now with only one hand.

Takeo's mind raced. There was no way he could stop the man, but the train—if he could warn the train! He could see its headlight now, far down the stretch of track. Scrambling to his feet, Takeo started to run down the tracks, his arms waving wildly, shouting at the train. The man in the train would see him. He must see him!

Jake Stock reached Tolliver a moment after the boy had started running down the tracks.

"Captain! Come on!"

The face that turned to him was contorted in fury.

"Captain!"

Tolliver's mouth worked soundlessly, and, as Stock started toward him, he clawed at the forty-five and swung it so that it pointed straight at Stock. He said nothing. Stock doubted that he was capable of speech.

Looking down the tracks, Stock could see the headlight growing larger, and the boy was running toward it. Then back to the man crouching on the track, the man who had once been a god . . .

"Goodbye, Captain . . ." He knew Tolliver had not heard. Tolliver was past hearing anything.

Stock wheeled and started after the boy. As he ran he could feel the pounding vibration on the tracks as the

210

train rushed toward them. The boy was a good thirty yards ahead of him. Stock and the train were racing to reach the boy first.

Twenty yards . . . ten . . .

Then the boy glanced over his shoulder and saw him— stumbling as he did and sprawling face down. As Stock made the leap, he knew for one heart-stopping instant that he and the train would reach the boy at the same time. He was caught in the glare of the headlight—heard the pounding of the locomotive—had one hand on the boy and was flinging him aside, then throwing himself after him . . .

He was clear!

On top of the boy, rolling away as the train roared past then, Stock caught a crazy, blurred glimpse of the locomotive, thought he saw the engineer, heard the whistle raised in a long piercing scream. Then he lay, face down, covering the boy's squirming body with his own, for he knew what would happen next.

Inouye saw someone running toward the train on the tracks, and he sounded the whistle to warn the fool that his train would be neither stopped nor slowed. He also saw the man who pulled the fool to safety, but he did not care. If he had killed them both, he would not have cared. It would have given him great pleasure to kill. Then he saw the other man, actually kneeling on the tracks. The world that night was inhabited by fools! Again he released the shrill command of the whistle—and again and again. The fool would not move!

Very well then! He pushed the throttle open as far as it would go, and his teeth bared in a savage, wolfish grin. He could hear the fireman shouting something, but he had no time to listen to him. Leaning out of the cab, he saw the man on the track look up. For one awful second their eyes met, and Inouye knew the man, and the man knew him—and they would know one another throughout all eternity . . .

Stock saw the locomotive as it reached Tolliver, and then he thought he heard a scream, but it was the whistle in one final piercing call—or was it really Tolliver's dying cry? Then the bomb went off. The locomotive seemed to lift for a moment and hang in midair. Then came the sound of the explosion, and the boiler went up in a shrieking, ear-splitting horror. The locomotive literally disintegrated, hurling pieces of itself in all directions.

The boy saw it too, and he was screaming as though the train were a part of himself. A smoking chunk of metal crashed to earth only a few feet from where Stock and the boy lay. Then the cars of the train jammed together, splintering like matchboxes which had been crushed by some giant fist.

One car, the last one, a freight car escaped the destruction. Stock saw it jump the track, careen crazily free of the holocaust, and finally come to rest about twenty yards from where they lay.

Then, miraculously, there was silence. It was as if someone had suddenly frozen the scene. Stock could hear his own heavy breathing. Even the boy lay still. As he climbed to his feet, still holding to the boy, Stock saw the Japanese in the door of the freight car. He was obviously a soldier, and he carried a rifle in his hands. As he saw Stock, he seemed to hesitate, then started to raise the rifle. Instinctively, Stock clawed for his forty-five, releasing the boy as he did. The Japanese leveled the rifle, and Stock

212

heard the shot, felt his leg go out from under him as though he had been kicked. As he fell he got off a shot. He missed! The soldier leaped down from the freight car and was running toward Stock, shouting something.

The thought flashed through Stock's mind that the soldier was trying to tell him something, trying to help him, but he could not take a chance. Jonathan Tolliver's words came to him as he raised himself on one elbow and aimed the forty-five.

You have to keep on, as long as there is an enemy to kill, you must keep on killing him . . .

He squeezed the trigger. This time he did not miss. The rifle flew from the soldier's hand, and he spun forward on his face. Stock pulled himself painfully to his feet, surprised to find he was able to stand. The soldier rolled over and turned his face toward Stock. There was a mute appeal in his eyes, and Stock instinctively moved toward him. Then he saw the Japanese's hand go inside of his jacket for a weapon. The forty-five roared again, and the tortured features were blotted out with crimson. The hand fell free of the jacket, bringing with it an object which lay on the ground just beyond the fingers which clawed blindly for it once and then were still.

The something was a rag doll, the head twisted on the limp body, the painted face turned upwards in the moonlight.

"Oh, my God!" It was a curse—and a prayer.

Stock looked around to find the boy. He was crouched a few yards away, watching Stock, his face a grotesque mixture of hate and terror.

"Get away from here!" Stock yelled at him, knowing he would not be understood. He waved one arm furiously at the boy. "For God's sake, get away from here!"

213

The bullet had evidently hit him in the fleshy part of his right thigh. The leg was beginning to feel numb, but he could feel the blood running down it. Cautiously he tried a couple of steps. He could walk, but whether or not he would be able to make it back to the boat was another question. And if he did, what would he find? The other men from the *Mudskipper* were nowhere to be seen. If they had made it back, they might have already shoved off. Still gripping the forty-five, he started after them. There was a throbbing, searing pain where the bullet had struck him, but he knew he must keep moving. If the boat were there! It must still be there!

He had reached the high grass when he looked back and saw the boy following him. He had the rifle which the soldier had dropped. Turning, Stock plunged ahead, keeping as low as he could. Once—twice he fell, and each time the pain shot upward like a knife.

He tried crawling, then dragged himself to his feet again and started to run as best he could. Once he lost sight of his pursuer, but then the boy came into sight again. He too was running, keeping pace with the wounded man. Then the sea was in sight, bathed in the brilliant moonlight, but there was no sign of the other men. Sobbing with the pain now, Stock stumbled on to the edge of the rocks. He could see nothing, and he knew he was beginning to black out. Whirling back, the relentless figure of the boy came nearer . . .

Takeo had never held a rifle before. He had snatched this one up instinctively, not knowing why he did it or what he would do with it. His world had been destroyed before his eyes, and all that he knew was that the man who had been responsible was now escaping. It was Takeo's duty to stop him. The rifle frightened him. It was so heavy, and he had heard the dreadful sound it made.

Still he held on to it as he tracked the man.

He saw the man reach the edge of the rocks—saw him look around—heard him crying aloud—and then he heard other voices answering from below. The man disappeared over the edge of the rocks, and Takeo ran toward that spot. Down below him he saw other men dragging the wounded man into a boat. They were going to escape! With a shrill cry of rage, he raised the rifle, trying to hold it steady as he pointed it down in the direction of the men in the boat.

Stock lost consciousness as he went down the rocks toward the boat. He was aware of John Barringer's voice shouting in his ear, and he came to in the rubber boat. Fighting to bring things back into focus, he pushed himself to a sitting position, clinging to Barringer's arm for support.

"He's got a gun!" It was Fritz Schroeder yelling, and Stock looked up where Schroeder was pointing. He saw the boy then, etched sharply against the sky. He saw the rifle, saw the flame leap from it, heard the sharp *crack* as it fired.

The bullet went far wide of the boat which was now in the surf, kicking up a spray of water.

Schroeder was kneeling in the bottom of the boat, taking aim with his submachine gun at the boy . . .

This one time, Tolliver! This one time you must be denied!

"No!"

The word tore from Stock, and he lunged at Schroeder, striking the weapon from his hands. The last words he remembered were his own. "He's just a kid! Just a kid!"

When he knew anything again, he was lying huddled in the bottom of the rubber boat. His trousers had been ripped away and the wound crudely bandaged. Beside him sat Finley Tatum, who had been hit in the shoulder by the shot from the Japanese who had surprised him and Schroeder and, in turn, had been killed by Schroeder.

"There she is!" Tommy Lyle was pointing. Stock pulled himself up to see the silhouette of the *Mudskipper* and the flashing signal from the submarine's bridge.

"Send a reply," he said. "Let them know we're here . . ."

"Mr. Stock . . ." John Barringer's voice was unsteady. "What do we say about him—about the Captain?"

Stock sat silently for several seconds, trying to find the answer. He remembered Tolliver as he had seen him last, and he remembered the other Tolliver he had known. Which man was Barringer asking about? Which man had been Jonathan Tolliver?

"Say—say the Captain went back to make sure the bomb was okay. He got the wires reconnected, but he couldn't get clear in time. He—he died bravely, doing what it was his duty to do—trying to destroy the enemy."

All right, Captain, now we are even—you and I.

He looked around at the solemn faces of the men in the boat. "Is that clear to all of you? The Captain died like a brave man—doing his duty."

They nodded silently. Jake Stock took one final look in the direction of the Hokkaido coast. He wondered if the boy still stood there. He wondered if that boy would ever grow into a man, and, if he did, would the man ever be able to erase the horror of that night.

Then he turned toward the *Mudskipper*. He could see the men on deck, ready to take them aboard.

The fish, Stock thought wearily, has returned to its proper home.

It was over.